# TERNA OF CARFORT

# Terna of Carfort

LILY O'REILLY

SERENDIPITY

First published in 2002 by
Serendipity
Suite 530
37 Store Street
Bloomsbury
London

*British Library Cataloguing-in-Publication data*
A catalogue record for this book is available from the British Library

ISBN 1-84394-021-3

Printed and bound by Alden Digital, Oxford

# Contents

CONTENTS

# CHAPTER ONE

# *Terna's Parents*

Terna Branton was born in Carfort in South County Galway, on the first day of November (All Saints' Day on the calendar) in the early nineteen hundreds. Stormy winds roared around the house, and the new member of the family screamed at her discomfort. The baby was fair with very blue eyes and a small face like her mother, a former Monaghan beauty. The Brantons were farming stock who had run Carfort for a few generations. Both of Terna's parents came from prosperous County Galway families and Honoria had travelled widely in her younger days.

Dick Branton had a chequered boyhood and early manhood. Both of his good parents had died within three hours of each other, when he was around eight years old, the eldest of six children. Such a situation can be more easily understood than explained, though the older relatives on his mother's side acted unbelievably kindly, by taking the most helpless children and rearing them in their own homes. But there still remained the task of minding the others – three – and this responsibility fell on young Dick's shoulders, until his sisters began to settle themselves from the age of eighteen and his brothers emigrated. Terna was the fifth child of Dick and Honoria who were opposites in character. The latter, with her natural superiority and mental stature, was out of place.

Carfort, at that period, was not so different from other houses in the parish, though the Brantons owned the greater part of the long valley that comprised rich, green fields and heathery stretches, as well as small paddocks. Their farm joined the two hundred acres that Dick's sister owned at one time. To the south west of Carfort is a

1

grand sweep of heathery hills with a lake in the centre, known as the Heather Lake. Many were the expeditions made to the top of those heights by the Branton children. It was in this lake that Terna waded in later years to pluck bulrushes and lilies. In Summer her group gathered berries off the heather, bilberries, perhaps. Usually, when the little travellers returned home after the three mile climb, Terna was the least tired.

Nature used to wield her brush skilfully over the landscapes of Carfort. As each season dawned, its beautiful hues, blending in harmony, were committed to the carpet of the valley. Bees and butterflies filled the warm spaces, and gay flowerets sprang from unexpected places in the boglands until early Autumn waved flags of gold and a tired green in the fertile fields. The mearing waters were dimpled by small fish that dived and darted at the bottom of them. Terna's family often enjoyed fresh trout for tea. Her brother, Will, was the fisherman of the family.

Branton's House was in a setting of sturdy trees, principally mountain ash, with big fields around. The carefully kept flower garden in front was good to see when blossoms were in full flush. The giant sunflower was a prime favourite with Terna's mother. This flower reared its face like a golden plaque in the middle plot of the garden. The violet-hued lilac looked half-shy, half-proud, in its own corner. It was in the lilac's shade that Tabby, the cat, used to stretch with feline grace. Sometimes Mrs Branton would lift her daughter Terna, take her to the rose arch and say: 'Do you hear that robin? He is saying: 'Te—ter—na, and calling *you*.' Terna, then, would try to remain with the robin and giggle with delight. The Brantons had two other daughters, Vena and Fay. Both girls were in striking contrast to Terna. They were brunettes. Marto, Jay and Will were intelligent, vigorous boys not afraid to turn their hands to anything.

CHAPTER TWO

# Terna's Early Years

Child of a perfect mother, Terna's heart and soul expanded in the joyousness of her tender years. She sang in her cot until she dropped off to sleep. With a pink toe tucked into her mouth, she filled the house with mumbled music, and tried to whistle like the birds whenever she went outside, but her gapped teeth prevented her from doing so. The heat of the Carfort sun sometimes proved too much for her, and she would grow dull and dispirited with it. The cool saw her bouncing with the vitality of her darker sisters again.

Terna's mother taught her to appreciate the beauties of Nature from an early age. It was broadly admitted by all that it was her lady mother who first turned her thoughts to aesthetic values. In the middle of a busy day in the old-fashioned house she would say a poem or passage from Robby Burns. She considered his work coarse but not vulgar. Terna watched her fine presence and did not miss the glad surprise that stole over her face now and then, something described later by herself:

> *The mist of bluebells matched my mother's eyes*
> *And the yellow of the dilly her hair's shade,*
> *And when her face showed glad surprise*
> *I thought of sunburst in a glade.*

Clouds began to gather on the Branton horizon after the birth of the youngest member of the family, Will, who was a year younger than Terna. Mrs Branton's health was surprisingly good. Stock died on the farm, crops and the weather were unsatisfactory. The tone of the heretofore genial family changed, from the pressures and fruitless efforts to improve circumstances, and Dick Branton was not averse to a glass of alcohol.

The mother bravely tackled her ever-growing duties, for her self-reliance and resourcefulness carried her through. 'What is, must be,' she would say, shaking her head sagely, and then gather her children round her at night to sing the songs that she loved so well, such as 'Oh! when will my countrymen learn to be sensible?' And also: 'Has sorrow thy young days shaded?' She had sung these songs in foreign places to her numerous friends, and she enjoyed having an audience again though her voice broke sometimes. Once, after a family concert, little Terna remarked to Fay: 'Our Mammy sings to hide the pain in her heart.' The Brantons saw a succession of bad years. Providence had endowed Terna; her mother found a special joy in her daughter's recitations, songs and mimicry.

Then a sad happening deprived the child of her usual gaiety for some time. On an evening when her mother was unavoidably absent the girl tried to hang a utensil over the big grate in the kitchen filled with live coals. Her older brothers and sisters were attending the Kilcross National School. As she leaned forward, the fire caught her wool frock and quickly spread to her left arm and side. The young child scarcely realized the extent, so there were no screams to attract her mother's attention; no shriek of innocent delight in danger. But luckily a neighbouring man passing from his work, minutes later, heard her first cry of pain, rushed in, rolled the child in his overcoat and set about quenching another small blaze with a bucket of water that was handy. This ensured her safety and he remained until her mother returned. Honoria was almost in need of a sedative with that. She stayed awake at night on purpose, for months, for fear the girl would grow over-heated and suffer as a consequence.

The marks of the burns were still on Terna, and she spared her left arm as its sinews were shorter than those of the right, and were to remain so. Time passed slowly and then she was treated like a visitor after that.

Things were no better on the farm in Carfort. Her father continued to meet the times and conditions with weary effort. Try as he would, he could not effect a change for the better. But Terna's safety helped to bring back the smile to her mother's face. The brothers and sisters made consistent progress at school, but it was quite apparent at this time that Marto was no lover of books or study. Serious Vena was a good student and seemed to be the queen of the school in Terna's eyes.

When the sun smiled in the Carfort valley Terna romped and gathered wildflowers in large bunches. Fay, who was her senior by two years, was her constant companion. After school, Fay dressed her in one of the beautifully laundered frocks which their mother provided. And they would set off together to the spacious woods on the Ponty estates less than a mile away.

The woods deserve a detailed description. Long colonnades of trees stand like dark barriers against the weather. Among them, happy woodmates meet, though there are no gentle deer beneath the trees, for the owner of the estate is gone away and it is divided among former workers and others. The remains of the late owner's place lie hidden in rhododendrons. Often stray cattle are heard calling through the woods, and long-tailed horses cool themselves in the heat under close, red-berried branches. It was in these woods that Terna and Fay sat making their plans. The girls would make wrappers of their pinafores and fill them with crab apples to make jam. Their mother was an excellent cook. Time concealed a secret from Fay, for in the distance, away in the hollows, stood the prosperous house of which she is mistress today. She little dreamed in those days that she was to marry her cousin, an only child.

Mrs Branton trained her other children to be tenderly careful of Terna. Going for a ride on old Rosie, the donkey, she reminded them with warning finger not to forget Terna's burns. In any kind of boisterous games the players would be admonished with: 'Mind Terna!' As far back as cradle days Will Branton developed ear trouble. His inner ear was affected. From a very hefty baby he became the opposite. He refused food and slept badly. The family doctor had told his parents that they would never rear him. But his mother refused to believe it and set about building him up, and with the exception of the affected ear, her son thrived under her care for years.

The time for Terna to begin her education finally arrived. She longed to accompany her brothers and sisters to school. On a May morning when the skies were white and blue Vena and Fay walked on either side of her to school followed by their mother's usual injunction to mind her. Dressed in white lace with her thick hair in several golden ringlets, she tripped rather than walked. At the school the newcomer was received well by the teachers. Her observant eyes took in her new surroundings. She was five and a half years old. Vena and Fay enjoyed having the responsibility of her. It made them feel grown-up before the other girls. As soon as the novelty of school life died away, Terna settled down and found it pleasant to obey the rules for little ones. Her teacher praised her from time to time. Learning was not difficult for her but some subjects bored her from the start. By the time she had reached second grade the Principal and other teachers decided to promote her two classes higher. Her fluent reading of a sixth standard book led them to believe that she was wasting her time, though her mother did not approve from the point of view of taxing her strength. When Terna herself was faced with homework as well, she began to slacken in her class. Her teachers were dismayed for they counted on her. Her mother worried. Sister Vena looked defeated. Terna offered no explanation, only lived from day to day doing her bit. Then, there followed a testy period for her and even her mother grew quite impatient. But all learning grew more and more distasteful to her. Always obedient, it came as a painful surprise when she obstinately refused to take any lunch, and fasted from eight a.m. to four p.m.

After her four o'clock substantial dinner she escaped into the fields either to fondle her pet goose or to run races with her pet kid that she had almost domesticated. In her imagination the eggs that her pet hen laid were of superior quality to those of the other hens. Still, with those distinguishing features and often with a show of spirit, her eldest brother stoutly maintained that 'Terna was the only angel in the house'.

Her sudden prankish inconsistencies amused rather than angered him. Whenever he would try to remonstrate with her she would spring on to his back to be carried all over the lawn. She excelled at high jumps and loved the three-legged race. Once Fay and herself got into a long bag and ran twice over a two-acre field. Suddenly they found that their feet were no longer hampered for the bag had given way at the bottom. Terna's screams of laughter could be heard a mile away for the girls finished the race with the bag drawn up loosely over them.

Earlier on, she had found two dead robins and brought Will to help her to bring them back to life. She stood aghast with pity and persuaded Will to take them to a haycock in their father's haggard and pray for their recovery, their ultimate revival! She was so disappointed when her child's faith went unrewarded! Later she ran from the swing between the ash trees to hide in prayer in her brother's pink room. She liked to pray alone and would always invoke the patron saints of the family.

# CHAPTER 3

# Successful Plans

Holiday-time heralded a run of freedom for Terna. To jaunt around on the farm machinery when her father allowed her, was her idea of enjoyment in the sunny season. She hid in the soft hay spread out to dry before being made into rows and cocks, and listened, fascinated, to the drone of a mowing machine in action, like the hum of multiple bumble bees. She usually had a full programme in vacation, doing the rounds of her relatives' homes. She visited her one maternal uncle in the parish of Cratton seven miles away. It was here that she feasted on green gooseberries and fell ill.

Her uncle, John Monaghan, was a sterling character and very kind. He had no sons and daughters to brighten his life and home, so his niece's visits were something to look forward to. He was engaged in farming and married late an elderly woman a mile from his own place. It was plain to see that he was Terna's favourite. For hours on Sunday he would stand before his old gramophone with the big horn and listen to records of his lifetime favourites, songs of his native land. Then Terna would have to regale him with scraps of her earlier recitations and school songs, adding her own comical bits to amuse him. Eventually, this uncle willed Jay all his possessions and, indeed, the latter proved to be a worthy successor, for while Terna was entertaining and kind, Jay was the more attentive to him.

All good times and things come to an end. Soon the hardy breezes of shorter evenings told Terna that school and lesson-time were stealing on her again. Around the re-opening, a wise person had advised Mrs Branton privately to be most understanding with her third daughter's continued aversion to home study. The speaker held the highest

8

opinion of Terna even while her teachers disapproved for the time being.

Early in September the much-discussed pupil surprised everybody concerned with her application to her work both at school and at home. Wonder of wonders! Her relatives seemed to enjoy a new lease of life. The wise adviser declared that she knew that Terna's lapse was only a passing phase. Terna, at nine, was an avid reader of children's stories. Even the time for homework became important. She never had to be reminded at all. And the change in the family fortunes were more easily accepted as a result. Her mother openly admitted so.

As Terna was a far-seeing child, her parents often asked her predictions of the family's undertakings. Her answers were mostly correct. It was an important time for her then, and for the next two years, for apart from writing simple prayers in her copy-book she composed little verses about fields, flowers, relatives, worldly weaknesses and the mistakes of others, the last with the understanding of one fifteen years older. Deep-down, Dick and Honoria Branton looked forward to her future achievements, especially when they came across the following on the back of an old receipt:

> *My father and mother are awful*
> *Always talking of caution*
> *Too much is no good*
> *It's not that in the wood.*
>
> *Terna Branton*

Expressions of her own, but none of them punctuated. Not until it dawned on her at around twelve years of age, after Vena and Fay taught her what they had to observe in their compositions. 'There are rules for writing,' Vena would warn her. 'The teachers say that rows of words make no sense unless they are punctuated.' So Terna soon learned about commas, full stops, colons and semi-colons. Though she grasped things quickly, she soon grew tired of the repetition necessary to retain them. She appeared to come into her own when her teacher asked the class to write a verse or two lines about birds. She wrote:

> *I saw half a dozen birds*
> *Not a feather on them stirred.*

9

Rhyming came rather easily to her. So much so that her mother ceased to wonder at the disappearance of the butter-paper from the tins every Saturday after churning. It was Terna who had been using it and who explained sweetly: "Twill spare you buying copies, won't it?' So the Brantons followed the usual routine and then it was time for Vena to finish at the local school. Marto had already left to help on the land, for he was the eldest son.

More changes were on. Terna decided that she would no longer attend the parish school. She had been covered with compliments, praise and respect until suddenly the reverse became the case. Words of ridicule stung her, discouraged her. So soon in life! After that she slipped back and no longer enjoyed attending, and even though she hated disappointing her mother, she made her plans and some weeks passed.

She started off on a Monday, as always, with Will. The morning was so fine that it seemed a pity to spend it indoors. But that was not the real reason that the girl handed Will over to two other boys passing to school when they all met at the fork of the road. But she thought again. She missed her brother so much that she ran after the scholars and persuaded him to turn back with her. 'Where?' Will asked. 'Home, is it?'

'Come on,' she urged, and never drew rein until they stopped at Suntry National School in the parish of Kildomey, three miles farther than the local one from their home.

The children arrived at 11.30, just an hour before lunch. It was an adventure for Will, who carried their two bags and did not seem to mind, but the rough road and the hills exhausted them. Terna knocked firmly on the heavy, closed door, taking in a flock of young geese at the same time, that arched their necks near her. Then the door of the solid building was opened by the strangely-sweet mistress of the school who thought it was the parish priest of Kildomey who had knocked. The lady received the children as if they were her own, and they, in turn, were led away by her manner. Terna claimed that that half-day in Suntry school was happiness itself. During lunch hour Will and herself, the two new pupils, as their teacher called them with delight in her face, set out for a short walk to see their surroundings. The school was smaller than the Kilcross building. It was situated in the heart of a high mountainous district where even summer breezes were enough to take one off one's feet.

The other pupils, twenty in all, were slow to make free on the new ones, but Terna and Will were soon fraternizing with them. The scholars were from Suntry and were rather slow of intellect, answering in a subdued, uncertain way. Young as she was she wondered at the average results on account of the small number and the perfect tuition given them. It was more like private tuition in her eyes. The teacher, Mrs Moran, never asked the arrivals who they were or where they lived until closing time. But as soon as they mentioned their surnames she recognized them and praised their parents. 'You are a god-send, dears!' She drew Terna aside and whispered, 'The average is low. I can lose the school.' Terna felt happier and useful at the words as she turned towards her parents' home and to reckon with her strict father. She knew there would be panic over their arriving an hour and a half late from school. She was correct.

As Will and herself approached they stood at the side entrance before they opened the green gate on to the palisade. 'We will tell the truth, Will,' Terna advised. At last they passed through the open front door and their mother waited, wondering, worrying ... 'Children! What happened?'

Terna explained everything, adding that they never wanted to go to Kilcross School again. Their mother gasped and then stiffened at the idea. It was no harmless escapade. 'Terna! What shall your father say?'

'Do not let him be angry with us. We love Mrs Moran. She is quiet and holy, Mother!' Then Will spoke. 'She told Terna that God sent us or she would lose the school.'

'Gracious! All that way out on your little feet!' Then the rest of the family arrived. Honoria expected that Dick would chastise the children and allowed them to speak first before they partook of a meal. Dick sensed something though he had been absent all day. His wife had an air of gravity as she looked at the children and then at him. She then served the meal and finally broke the news. Wonder of wonders again! Dick Branton was favourably disposed to the idea! Apart from the extra miles he could not fault it as he already knew the reputation of Mrs Moran as a teacher. At his ready approval the children looked as if they had got a ticket to Heaven. Terna began her homework immediately with a renewed interest. 'You are great, Daddy!' she told him. 'Mother and you understand everything and everybody.' Then she predicted, 'You will not be sorry.'

So the two youngest of the Brantons set out each day for Suntry, happily determined. Most days they took a short-cut and found themselves on the school grounds before the local children put in an appearance or the only teacher arrived with her key. Terna's going to Suntry was an important step in her young life. Learning was an easy joy. She revelled in the peace and spaces and the simplicity of the people. She loved the dashing streams and little lanes, the white-washed cottages, the neat women who went about their daily work with willing hands. An old resident of the place once called her a skylark on account of her early arrival day after day. Other people mentioned the way she would greet them and some called her 'Little Lady Branton'. Another addressed her as 'Miss Kilcross'! And an eccentric old lady asked her fairly and squarely from time to time 'why she walked and talked with the locals who had humps on their backs, and who used to work for her father, that decent man! while he lasted. And if it were true that she helped the teacher correcting copies during school hours?' Terna answered with a delighted smile only and the enquirer moved away reminding her to keep smiling for she had lovely teeth.

A well-respected figure at that time was the Reverend Thomas Hogan who visited the Suntry school regularly. Both Terna and Will liked him. He was a man of spirit and of a benevolent nature. He always impressed on the children that life was a stepping-stone only. Then he would sing with Terna until she hoped they would cease as long standing tired her. Moore's melodies were his choice.

It was soon apparent to the Brantons that poor Will's ear trouble was becoming acute. Terna grew sad at heart. It was a cloud on her happiness, that he could not attend regularly in cold weather. She started to write prayers and to say them on the way to and from school for him.

Two years passed away with a regular programme that was never monotonous to Terna, and then the question of secondary education for her was discussed by her parents. It appealed to her, so she went to the little pink room to state her case. It was a brief prayer but well said, and out of the blue she found once again that her plans were about to materialise and that her mother was already writing for prospectuses to different schools. So Terna left her childhood home for a boarding school in her native county with her teacher's words ringing in her ears: 'You're an extraordinary child and you will do

12

very well unless you are undermined.' The words gave her courage and panache in her new world. She embraced it with ready respect for the nuns in authority, loved meeting new faces, enjoyed her studies, walks and recreation and rose to it enthusiastically when she was named for a part in a play: *The Easter Fire on the Hill of Slane.* The particular part that she did enraged a member of the audience so much that he demanded later that she should not repeat it in the event of another staging of the play. 'It was not suitable for her,' he complained, 'a rough man's part. Not suitable at all.' But Terna never minded as long as she was acting. As week followed week in her confined life she began to suffer from headaches and found it difficult to concentrate, and even to retain what she learned. She thought of Kilcross. The Principal looked perplexed, the French teacher smiled with warm understanding for she liked Terna and expected her to progress. Before she was six months learning French the same teacher asked her to help students who had difficulty with the subject even though they had studied it for two years before she began.

Terna had keen perceptions and she loved nuns. She genuinely regretted their not winning a Cup on her answering with Irish idiomatic phrases on account of her learning the phrases elsewhere. No hatchet faces and prominent, glaring eyes on her for the smallest mistake! Most of the time, Terna decided that young nuns looked like lambs on a sunny day in Carfort, and were truly the soul of holiness all through. The girl often found comfort in her mother's words about people: 'Take them as they come.' Even a young one, though not yet up against the battle of life or engaged in it, can benefit from a wise, kind word.

Literature was Terna's whole delight. She loved composition, in French, English or Irish. At oral examinations she excelled, and occasionally a nun requested her to read her work to the older classes as well as her own. She often felt conspicuous and shy when she would stand beside the nun and face the classes. Likewise, when an elderly member of the community termed her a genius to her sister Fay who called to see her on her first birthday there. In her steady progress and with frequent headaches she often visualized the airy expanse of Carfort where she could be alone to inhale; to listen to the music in a bubbling stream; to hear trout dash in brown waters; to see a cold countryside waiting to be warmed by the sun; and to wade once more in the cool waters of the heather-bound lake.

Carfort was resting under a foot of snow when she arrived home for Christmas. Her people looked to her coming with keen pleasure, and had already arranged a programme, just as they had not forgotten *un grand gateau sucré avec quatorze chandelles* on her fourteenth birthday. After greetings, her first enquiry was for her Suntry teacher whom she visited and found suffering from rheumatism. Mrs Moran commented on the mousy shade of her hair and on her height.

Apart from the Christmas programme the girl turned down an invitation by her brothers to make snowmen. The cold was intense in that region and she remained indoors quite a lot. The time passed pleasantly and reopening day came with goodbyes and an ache in her heart because her mother looked haggard and pale.

Apart from walking there was nothing else to do but study, study, study. There were no games. And Terna's headaches never forgot to come back. But she was receiving good news of her mother's better spirits and this helped her noticeably. She could apply better, and once her French teacher said, '*Votre pronunciation est parfait.*' The school routine went on, broken only by visits and vacation. And she was growing up. Her brother Jay teased her constantly over her reedy look and her ringlets that never needed twisting. And that she resembled Aristotle in repose! or Wordsworth musing on a stretch of bog in Carfort! She enjoyed being teased for she had a strong sense of humour. She called her scoffers and critics: God's other children. Double-faced people she could not stand. She praised all nuns for their singular services to humanity, but whether she would finish her course lay with herself.

## CHAPTER 4

# *Important Changes*

The terms flew and then Terna was home in Carfort intending never to go back. Attitudes, words and actions of others induced this. She made up her mind very quickly as to which course she would adopt. And never had the Carfort valley looked so inviting. The woods were gay with different blossoms. The curlew's call like a complaint was heard. Sheep and lambs dotted a paddock though there were few of them. The water of the lake was like a sheet of blue glass and the skies bluer than usual. Breezes kissed the growing corn making it wavy. The potato crop, so far undamaged by blight, was dark in the distant corner of the field. Sturdy stalks stood strong and erect with a promise of a plentiful yield. A welcome change from the opposite of the year before. The family was happily engaged at the farming pursuits for some months, so Terna turned her hand to general housekeeping.

On one rare occasion, having made a double round of scones, she stepped to the robin arch, as she had decided to call the rose arch of happy memory, and let her natural inclination be satisfied to the full. As she watched the golden glints and wafting motion of the light leaves she was filled with a mounting admiration and she expressed it: 'These moments! Oh! that they could last!' Then she turned into the kitchen, thankful that no one heard her, and wrote the names of two little verses that she meant to write: *After the Rain* and *Sabbath Peace*.

The Brantons were well aware of her budding propensities for this work. Her mother just stood and wondered about it all. Her daughter's rhyming couplets always amused her, especially the speed with which

15

they were composed and written. Terna appreciated the opinions of those who were qualified to judge her amateur work, and loved reading the literary criticism in the newspapers and books.

The harvest return was tremendous. Dick Branton expected to have several stacks in his haggard. The humming of the different machines made a monotonous music and reminded the workers of past progress in Carfort. Their mother served good fare, properly cooked and the family was in great tone at the end of Autumn. And better still, honest labour was to be amply rewarded. Prices for foodstuff and livestock soared. Terna's brothers attended the fairs and fetched decent prices for their animals. Worthy of special mention was the purchasing of a very becoming suit with a beautiful, shady hat for the eldest Miss Branton. Though Terna considered the hat too large, so it almost covered Vena's face.

That Autumn Terna penned two more short compositions: *Autumn* and *Down Here*. She chose a secluded sanctum to do this and had the others wondering as to her whereabouts. The sanctum, wrongly called 'The Isle' lay where a narrow river that seldom went dry hurried between rocks and stones covered with moss. Layers of fine sand filled its sides. Bluebells, primroses, daisies and fern grew on its banks.

*And bluebells grew in mild profusion in the Isle up there*, taken from *Breeze-borne thoughts*. The sunshine escaped through overhanging boughs. On both banks overhead, thick hazel leaves clung together, covered with nuts. At a bend of the river, a dashing waterfall washed the largest rock. In such places Terna craved for time and inspiration to follow up the work that she valued, that she knew was part of her … like breathing. And she often tore up her jottings and watched them sail away on the clear waters.

Winter's nip was already in the air when a faraway cousin announced his intention of spending a holiday in Carfort, so due preparations were made. Mrs Branton's hospitality was well known since the day she settled in that rural spot, having spent fifteen years in one of the largest cities in the world. Soon Cousin Jim arrived. He was a very tall, lean young man with deep brown eyes and raven-black hair. He had a pleasant face in repose but when he spoke a hardness that resulted from momentary nervousness spread over it and changed its expression. At the time he was contemplating a matrimonial engagement. The Brantons thought he was too young for such a serious step but never said so. Jim spent a month in Carfort where young and old helped to make his visit enjoyable. During his stay he met another cousin of the family. But the highlight of his stay was the visit to the city of Galway with his Uncle Dick. They dined and wined at the best hotel there, relaxed at the beach, purchased some gifts and returned home. They then tumbled into bed to sleep off their exhilaration. As his stay was drawing to a close, Terna entertained him at night in the parlour. So did Vena, and Fay who was always ready for witty exchange.

The restlessness of the teenager was beginning to show on Terna. Even though she led a full, useful life she longed to get away to view different scenes and to meet people. She decided to become a nurse. This notion was firmly ruled out by her parents. Her mother reminded her sternly about her weaker left arm and its short sinews. Her father reminded her of a nurse's heavy work in wards and the strain of night nursing. By degrees, the girl was won over. She filled her spare moments with creative work. Knitting filled her evenings and the short days and the long nights seemed to fly.

# CHAPTER 5

# *Romance Beckons*

In mid-winter the skies over Carfort were green, and Carfort itself was white with layers of snow and hoarfrost. The snow remained in the valley long after it had settled in the hills. In the moonlight it made a picture worth remembering. The house and out offices appeared twice their size, crystal places hanging with diamonds when the icicles formed on them. Now and then from a stable came the soft neigh of a mare. Calm-eyed cows chewed the cud comfortably. In the corner of the farmyard well-fed fluffy poultry dreamed of chickens. A shaggy haired, faithful collie kept guard outside the henhouse against possible invasion by hungry foxes. Geese and ducks cackled and quacked at the other end before they decided to settle down.

Terna's parents read to each other. They were both clever, and their sons and daughters respected and admired their father's way of killing a wet day. He would take a few interesting books to the parlour and remain there for hours. The couple retired early in Winter. They were believers in regular hours.

Just then Vena was sentimentally interested in a young Protestant who lived on a large farm a few miles away. Knowing that she should receive early opposition from her family, she decided to meet him secretly. Another young man who lived near Carfort was attracted to Terna. He was older by three years, with powerful shoulders and physique. Some girls liked his masculinity. But to Terna, the dark giant was by no means desirable enough to marry. Nevertheless, he broached the subject of matrimony on a very early Spring evening only to receive a prompt and casual refusal while her eyes rested on the new green of the hedgerows, after which he presented her with a beautiful encased silver medal on a chain as a keepsake. Terna had a negative reply time after time, so he decided to remain a bachelor and never went back on that decision.

With the lengthening days Carfort began to hum. Cousin Jim was arriving again for a stay with the cousins whom he liked best. It was now early May. The earth and the sky seemed to meet in a sunny embrace. The month touched the wildflowers with her loveliest hues and soft showers fell to freshen them. Young grasses enriched the fields. Pheasant and grouse called from the moory side of Carfort; the lake slopes receiving the sounds. And in the boggy stretch, bonfires blazed in preparation for turf-cutting. The tough heath had to be removed before the banks could be skinned.

Jim arrived at the time that his engagement had been officially announced and he had reason to be happy in the Branton circle, for most of them extended invitations to his fiancée and her relatives. So ended another perfect holiday for him. As the Brantons grew older there were not so many restrictions on them. Each one of them had his set of friends. Their parents enjoyed the new developments while they themselves were settling down to grow old gratefully. It must be said that before Jim left, he sauntered with the girls through the big fields of Carfort, on to the main road that led off from a country lane near the village of Garmana. The evening was lively. A cuckoo from a wayside tree and young birds chirped happily as they passed. Even though the walkers were on familiar ground they had a certain sense of adventure. Vena stopped to pluck a bouquet of primroses for herself, and the others strolled on. A happy silence fell between them. Then, suddenly, at a crossroads the substitute for a parish hall came into view. It was a square of cemented ground, sixteen feet by sixteen feet or so. The young people usually gathered on summer evenings to dance the hours away there. It went under the name of 'The Flag'. Jim thought it a novel idea and joked about the possible attack of midges while the couples were dancing 'the light fantastic'. Vena had rejoined the party by then and a young, uniformed male figure appeared on a bicycle also. It was a friendly meeting for the men had met before, as the uniformed stranger was a member of the Police Force. They had met at a race meeting. Peter Canning was the policeman's name and Jim made no delay in introducing his cousins. Terna was well impressed by the stranger. He was a composed, handsome, young man of between twenty and twenty-one who talked with a very responsible air and reliability.

After much small talk and exchanging views the cousins joined the dancers and never felt the night close in. When it was time to return home, Peter accompanied them for almost a mile of the road walking beside his bicycle and next to Terna. She chattered animatedly with him and he, undoubtedly, enjoyed her clean gaiety, and before he departed he extracted a promise from her that they should meet again. And Terna herself was surprised at her readiness to see him. The other dark man was now a fading ghost. Then it dawned on her that Jim had mentioned meeting Peter before and that explained their familiarity. And the fact that Peter wore a uniform did not enhance him in her eyes for she hated uniforms of any class.

Anyway a few days after that saunter and dance the appointed meeting came off and was a decided success. Peter was a worthy person. Though sometimes the image of the darker man holding a revolver with threatening attitude entered her mind and amused more than vexed her. By this time Vena and her Protestant friend had drifted apart. Perhaps it was on account of their different denominations, perhaps it was not. The summer lingered late that year and so did Terna and Peter. The girl mentioned leaving home less and less. They walked and talked together and spent every available moment at entertainments, far and near. Peter never danced and she was not so fond of it either. And as the months passed rumour soon had it that there was an understanding between the two. So nobody wondered when Peter slipped a five-stone engagement ring on her finger on her next birthday. Deep down Terna knew that she had taken a step in the right direction. By that time she had met and approved of some of his relatives and friends and so decided to keep her engagement secret for some time for her father's opinion of the life she would lead later was not encouraging. Nobody but Fay was informed of it.

This really pained Terna as she disliked to practise any deception under her parents' roof. Paternal wrath she expected. She did not expect to be surprised as once before. And had her sweet mother been informed of her engagement to Peter the most likely thing would be that she should repeat it to her husband. Fay, however, proved to be the exception rather than the rule regarding women and secrets. *She never revealed anything.* Terna's ring was carefully concealed in a small drawer in her dressing-table and worn only when away from the house. On many occasions she felt mean and secretive in the family.

So far, engagements and marriages were abstract subjects at home. The Branton daughters were plainly not interested in settling young. After Terna's engagement she turned up her ringlets and wore them like earphones on either side. Peter thought that her new hair style was not becoming to her at all. He said her round face appeared sharp in profile and her mother missed her ringlets.

One evening as Terna was making preparations for a car journey Vena noticed that she dressed extra carefully and stayed at her side to see her finish her toilet. Then came the embarrassing moment that the younger girl dreaded – slipping on her ring. After lifting it from its case she sidled to a window in order to act unseen but Vena soon detected the brilliant gems. There and then the affianced one told the truth when she observed the kindly, enquiring looks of her sister who sank into a chair, unbelieving. Terna engaged! Little Terna, the baby of the family but one. Clear incredulity was registered on her face, and she enquired with concern if Terna had informed her mother. The time was slipping and Terna replied a trifle impatiently: 'Becoming engaged is not a crime.' She turned and left the room with the ring still in its box. Vena sat down to the cloud of her thoughts at the step her sister had taken on her own initiative without consulting anybody. Unlike Fay, Vena went directly to her mother and blurted out the facts when Fay happened to be in the parlour.

Honoria Branton barely listened to the speaker but believed all, eventually, when Vena informed her that she had actually *seen* the sign of the happy bondage on the newly-affianced Terna. Their mother remained tactfully silent that night and requested them to be the same. Fay had unusual grimaces of disbelief until she said goodnight.

"What is the world coming to at all?' the father of the family asked at the breakfast table next morning. There was a prolonged stare at Terna who never raised her eyes from the juicy rasher she was manipulating.

'Terna, your father is speaking,' and the girl smiled both bravely and shyly at her mother.

'We hear that children should consult their parents on important matters,' Dick thundered across the table. 'You are engaged to be married to a stranger, Terna!' His voice rose. 'The Tom, Dick or

Harry, whatever you call him; I have not even a nodding acquaintance with him.'

'Your father is right and naturally upset,' pleaded the mother while the rest of the family agreed tacitly and waited for further parental disapproval which flowed easily. 'Do you give a thought to your future?'

'Of course I do ... Peter is so reliable.'

'A man in uniform, only a policeman!' groaned her eldest brother.

'And not that healthy looking, either,' Vera added with eldest-sister gravity.

'Oh, dear!' sighed Mrs Branton, 'the sky may be your roof, some day. Terna! Dick! Children! Please return that ring, that ring that was pushed on your finger by a stranger; it should not have been done that way.'

Terna rose and stood by her mother's chair, fumbling for words. But her mother's expression was enough, she was not helpful.

'But Peter *has* land as well as his salary,' the loved and loving one pleaded in a low voice.

'And where?' they pressed. 'In a dream?'

'In the County Westmeath, east of Westore.' She grew impatient then, 'and he does not smoke, or drink, and ... and ... everybody says that ... that he is a saint.'

Dick raised a finger. 'A paragon, I see.' He was sarcastic and Terna was hurt and fell silent and pale.

As they finished breakfast Marto spoke. 'Are you ill. Terna?'

Fay answered for her. Terna was too moved to speak, looking really like the youngest of the family. 'Terna is not ill. Not a bit of it,' Fay said, 'she may be contemplating marriage at the moment.'

'A big step,' he said. He was worried. 'Well,' he declared finally, 'as Terna is a girl with her head on her shoulders, I hate to say yes or no.'

Suddenly it all became too much for Honoria who reminded the girl that she did not believe that her daughter could have so much secrecy, and then, maternal to a degree, she said: 'What you want to do, you will do, I suppose.' At the words, Dick left the house quickly. A minute later he looked in, still angry. 'You have not my consent, Terna! Give back that ring! We can tell the world that your engagement is only a teen-age escapade – just a boy-and-girl affair.'

CHAPTER 6

# *The Engagement Continues*

A few days later, Terna had just come from 'The Isle' where she had written some lines with another mention of her mother. Vena and Fay smiled as she entered the kitchen. They were busy and she took up her knitting. Four eyes sought her finger, her bare finger as they thought. Then Vena evenly enquired if she had informed Peter Canning of their suggested disruption, and the engaged girl replied that she had not mentioned it and that in any case their mutual feelings would not be affected.

'Do you like Peter, Vena?' she began.

'No.'

'Why.'

'Because he is too perfect.'

'And what is your opinion, Fay?'

Fay pondered. 'I think that he is the type of person who would always plough his own furrow.' All three sisters laughed.

'By the way, when is Peter coming here?' Vena asked.

'Oh, well, considering that Father refused to acknowledge his friendly salute yesterday it ought to be very clear to us that Peter will not be too anxious to come − not to mention the outburst recently against him!' Vena and Fay looked concerned then and she went on, 'Not until I invite him, anyway. And that may not be for ages, for we are putting off marriage for a few years.'

Vena gasped. 'Gracious! when I meet the right one I will take him along to the altar at once.'

'Oh! you mean to choose and decide very much later on, as I do,' Fay said.

'Exactly, Fay!' She gestured funnily. 'Let the littlest Branton but one step it out!'

The girls worked quietly until the easing cadence of birds and the slow withdrawal of the sun showed that it was evening. They relaxed for a time and then the senior girls left. Terna's mind was busy, though. She knew well that her father's ire would not abate very quickly, if at all. But she remained true to Peter and herself. The couple planned pleasant outings in the fine afternoons, and even though Peter was stationed nine miles away in Sealwell, he never failed to turn up no matter what the weather was like.

Engagements are expected to be exciting affairs, but with Peter and Terna nothing glamorous or glorious came to colour their lives. With mutual consent they walked, talked and read together. Peter had an interest in the Irish language at the time. Sometimes they attended sporting fixtures, horse shows, racing and tracks. There was always an exchange of presents on birthdays and other times throughout the year.

Peter left each year for his home nearly a hundred miles away in the east of Ireland, and Terna always felt happy about this well-earned rest after all the long journeys to and from Carfort. She had been invited time and time again to meet his relatives but declined to do so, calling it a deferred pleasure. At such times Terna threw herself into her work and waited for the absent one's letters.

Even in days, Dick Branton had decided that remonstration would be utterly useless in the case of Terna's secret engagement. Though he promised himself to keep an adamant exterior, he knew he was softening inside. He liked Terna and regretted the fact that she was avoiding him. It hurt him in some way and all his paternal dignity called for some form of redress, and Terna herself was maintaining that those who love have rights and swore that she would enjoy his mortification later when he would be compelled to listen to Peter's praises being sung by all and sundry in and around Carfort.

During their engagement the happy pair attended a military dance. They made a foursome with Vena and her escort. Non-dancing Peter confined himself to the cardroom whenever Terna danced. The dance was held in a Castle some fifteen miles from Carfort. Peter looked better in plain clothes and Terna wore a white silk frock. She enjoyed meeting some of her old pals of Secondary School days there. This happened: during an interval and just before the dancers started again, a visiting gent at the Castle with an insipid face persisted in growing familiar with Terna, danced with her and then invited her to supper which offer she declined gracefully, explaining about Peter in the card room. Shortly after this Peter was walking slowly on the main road past a certain farm, when a volley of stones was fired at him from behind a hedge. He was scared stiff but luckily escaped unhurt. When be told Terna about the ambush and its location she suspected a young man with hate in his eyes and a deep jealousy.

CHAPTER 7

# *Problems at Carfort*

The Brantons of Carfort had now fully accepted the fact that Peter Canning was to remain a fixture. The parents had deduced from Terna's attitude of growing independence that she was not building herself a house of sand but one of solid stone. And the fact that she had regained all her old vivaciousness and animation gave them a happier outlook.

With the passing years conditions had not improved so much in Carfort. As usual, clever Honoria Branton, who had now many grey hairs among the gold, practised the strictest economy. Gradually, the fields were becoming bare, bare white plains full of scutch grass. No plaintive bleat of lamb calling its dam, no great cattle or young calves, or spirited horses neighing in their freedom. There were, however, three cows always there, one of which was to cause much sadness to Terna. One evening her father was trying unsuccessfully to physic that sick cow and he called her to help him raise the animal's head. Though dressed for an outing in her best apparel, she willingly assisted. As the cow, Bessie, rejected the contents of the carafe-like bottle totally, Terna suggested that they try her with a slice of turnip instead, slipping it into her mouth there and then with much patting on the sick animal's neck. The beast was too ill to swallow it. Bessie, the mother of many calves, died in a few minutes. Dick pushed her head aside on a pillow of hay. 'Poor Bessie,' Terna cried. Then she became vehemently brave. 'It is all right Dad! Bury her. There is always the chance of another.' After it she flew back to the little pink room to convert her emotions into a prayer and stayed home that evening.

Rent and rates had to be met on the Carfort farm or else sell it.

26

To part with an old place was hard to consider. The young Brantons, acting on their parents' advice, never emigrated. They were clever and industrious, certainly, but their mother, in particular, hated the idea of their settling outside Ireland. It was almost a stigma in her eyes. At this time Marto had the strength of a young lion. The gentle Jay had already been adopted by his equally kind and moderate uncle in Cratton.

Though unusual for him, Dick, at one time the most prosperous and forward looking farmer in his place, now became rather dispirited. And to add to it, Will's ear condition was pronounced 'chronic' by the doctors. His mother was so attached to her youngest son that she felt that no one had power to ruin him on her. She believed in something within herself that had kept him alive up to then. And despite Will's ailment, he kept the ball rolling in Carfort. He sang in his rich tone while he ploughed, and seldom worried, even about failing health. The family made every honest effort on the homeground to escape from the financial slough and no avenue to independence was left unexplored. There were now seven adults in the place. And there was a regular source of income through the annual setting of some of the land.

The farmer who grazed the land on the eleven months' system lived about half a mile as the crow flies from Brantons. He was about forty-seven years, and was supposed to have a lively interest in uncanny proceedings. One of these: before he would part with money he would always make sure to nip off a corner of notes to keep, then spit on each note (or cash) paid out. Dick never showed his embarrassment. The man never stood in church or chapel and believed in one world only, the ground under his feet. Yet, strange to relate, he never saw a wildflower but he lifted his hat with raised eyes and transformed face, leaving one wondering if it were the same face.

Another prospective grazier discovered that Carfort was in difficulties, difficulties of an urgent nature, so he made a proposal to its owner. Bargain would be a better word. He suggested taking about twenty acres of the best land, for a few years together. This would not be considered at all, under any circumstances. Terna once commented that the first man's favourite occupation was accumulating money for its own sake. All in all, it must have been galling to Dick Branton to see the average offspring of his former workers making shrewd offers to him.

One beautiful April evening while the Brantons were having tea they noticed a man approach on horseback. Chance must have directed his steps to Carfort for on that evening something more than cousinship developed between Fay and himself. As Honoria Branton saw their regard for each other ripen, into more she became duly worried. Cousins' mistakes. Loving to their later detriment?

After a year's constant companionship, however, Fay and Jock decided to remain apart to test whether they could live without each other or not. As in Terna's case with Peter, parental, well-meant interference was not missing. The parting was to last a month, but after three weeks Jock turned the knob on the front door noisily and rushed in declaring that there was nobody else in the world for him but Fay. Of the two young people Fay would have proved to be the stronger. Though she missed him, she did not pine for him.

Then Jock declared, too, that he was not one to tie a girl down with an engagement ring too soon. He approved of Fay getting around in mixed company and enjoying herself, but to keep her Jock was outspoken, with the heart of a lamb. He joked happily.

'No ring, yet, Fay,' he said, 'I do not want you to feel half-married.' Jock had a half-whimsical expression while Peter could be called serious and composed.

In all the rejoicing the news of the decent Cratton uncle's passing saddened all. Honoria rushed to her son's side and looked after everything. Terna was consolation itself to everybody, reminding them that all are born to die. Her uncle had been suffering from a peptic ulcer for years and his wife was a kindly woman all through. Unfortunately, he had not a chance to attend to his financial settlements, so he died intestate. This meant that Jay had to administer to the place.

Terna missed her uncle keenly. She was now close on twenty years of age. Peter was her senior by three years. He was lucky to be allowed to stay in Sealwell where he was a general favourite with all classes. Once, a daughter of the Protestant Dean of Kilcross, who ardently admired him, said that he was born to be a clergyman. An old-age pensioner's wife thought that he had a face like a judge. Another woman remarked that he was sincerely friendly for a 'foreigner'. A local farmer was of the opinion that he was either a saint or the other thing. Terna enjoyed this.

## CHAPTER 8

# *Developments*

Terna had now the mind of a woman. She was fully mistress of herself and very secure in the affections of Peter. And inwardly, she resented her father's sneaking indifference to Peter's existence – even though his ring was worn more often now over a period of twelve months. She decided to get rid of that situation and waited for the season of goodwill to dawn before she acted.

New Year's Day was near and the family expected guests. Terna announced that Peter should be among them. Nobody was enthusiastic or open, so she wrote a letter of invitation to him and sped away to post it. In it she added a postscript that the party was to be given *specially* for him. She lied because she had grown sick and tired of the effort that was called for on Peter's part to hide the hurt at being ignored both publicly and privately. So she waited eagerly for the fruition of her plan. Occasionally, members of her family would gloat over the coming guests and discuss their characteristics, how *who* was to be introduced to *whom* and the guests who should avoid each other.

On the evening of the entertainment Terna walked to the end of the long avenue to meet Peter and to accompany him to the house. And then usher him into the paternal presence! It was not easy ... Dick made no pretence of being over-pleased to see him, but Terna's natural thoughtfulness more or less covered up this fact. In a few minutes she led him to the very comfortable parlour where her mother received him with sincere charm and perfect courtesy. He impressed her. Peter felt happy and excited, so much so that Terna was able to forget the incident outside as they approached the front door when

29

he tripped over one of the fancy stones surrounding a flower pot and fell forward. He stayed several hours and mixed freely with the company, finding none of them snobbish. His future father-in-law he left strictly to himself. The occasion served to make him even fonder of Terna. He left Carfort referring to the striking similarity of Terna and her mother.

Peter left his barracks soon after on a pilgrimage to Our Lady of Lourdes' shrine in France. He travelled with a group of men. His going made news around peaceful Carfort and further. There was a snag, however, that marred the enjoyment of the tour. With cards, he wrote *two* letters only from his hotel in Paris – one to Terna and the other to his mother in Westore. His mother replied instantly while Terna's letter remained unanswered. This supposed negligence on Terna's part openly peeved Peter and he repeatedly made warm references to his mother's loving attention afterwards.

The cause of the *supposed* neglect on Terna's side was that he had stated in the letter that he was to *leave* the hotel on the day he posted it. He took some time to forget his disappointment even though explained. He had so looked forward to receiving a letter from her, and in France at that.

Fine weather came to Carfort after a spell of icy blasts and rain. Soon Spring had set the heart of Earth fluttering. Tiny, delicate flowers appeared on the land. Young things hopped and gambolled. There were rows of gorse like golden ditches in the distance that looked bright and inviting. Birds were astir in the hedges. Even the winter ravaged robin held up its head and sang. Here and there, little tufts of soft glass appeared. Odd cuckoo calls surprised the passer-by. Lambs looked as if they had fallen from the sky, so tiny were they in the wide, empty fields.

Will had a great interest in horses – not from the gambling viewpoint but for their use and beauty. He was mightily proud of a promising colt that his father had just bought and which he meant to break-in himself. It took over an hour for the family to decide on a name for the splendid animal. Some few were mentioned and the least appealing of all to Terna, chosen. To call a horse after a *duck* sent her into paroxisms of laughter. For *Sheldrake* was the name.

Sheldrake was a dark bay with long, flowing mane and a noble head. He was bred. Dick had another older animal, a red mare with a white stripe on her motherly face. Dolly was looked on as the hack of the farm. The mare had to be sold later to meet expenses and Dick parted with her reluctantly. The same party still continued to stock the best part of Carfort at a very moderate outlay, and took full advantage of the fact that the setter had to yield under financial pressures, even with seeming satisfaction. Good Honoria anxiously hoped that things would take a turn for the better, so that Carfort could pay its own way.

Like a bolt from the blue a party of strangers arrived at Brantons. They were elderly men and women – five in all. The lady received them with a polite, though distant, courtesy. The travellers did not disclose their identity for a considerable time and the atmosphere was strange. Then, suddenly, one of them, the eldest, stretched out his hands to Honoria. 'Ah! You do not remember Nicholas.' He was an old friend of her family who had been more familiar with the rest of them than he had been with her, owing to her absence overseas for years from the age of seventeen. She was deeply moved when she recalled the name, Nicholas Dunphy. The gulf of years seemed to vanish and she was back again in the home of her youth where her fond father and mother lavished love and kindness on her. She saw in retrospect the dark sister who had married the brother of Lady Grayle, and on becoming a convert to Catholicism, broke with his family and their custom of proselytism; the few years she lived with her sister and brother-in-law in their home in South Galway – 'Ash Lodge' – before she decided to leave Ireland.

All the Brantons extended a warm welcome to Nicholas Dunphy and his friends. When, at last, the party rose to go home, the mother told the story of Nicholas's life. He had been a solicitor in his early years and fancied an only daughter of a rich family. The couple would have married had his mother not taken over the arranging and re-arranging of their lives and all matters. He erred in allowing her to overrule all his inclinations. A critical friend remarked that her son had been bought by her rather than have been born of her, she loved him so fiercely, her all, her only treasure on earth.

Once when Nicholas bought his chosen one to her home, his enraged parent gave full vent to her jealousy and indulged in a maniacal fit of self-pity, even striking the girl in the face. The fiancée fainted witnessing such a scene. Later, the well-bred girl parted with him forever and the man fell ill and morbid, and then disappeared, never even coming to his mother's funeral. She was supposed to have shed tears of sorrow on her deathbed. Poor Terna was glad to hear the end of the story.

When the Brantons saw that old methods of farming were not paying they decided to turn to pig and poultry rearing on a large scale. Fay took over the turkeys and geese. With the increase of poultry came an increased egg yield. Will helped out by having more tillage. Oats were necessary to keep fowl in laying conditions. Litters were taken to the market regularly and sold. Year's end saw a substantial increase in Honoria's hands. The heavy Rhode Island Reds and beautiful Buff Orpingtons as well as white Leghorns charmed Terna. She loved the cackling symphony when a dozen hens announced the birth of an egg together. On one occasion she described fowl basking in ashes in the sun as 'pampered dowagers enjoying their leisure'. When a huge, heavy sow came into view she said that 'the animal had the expression of an elderly contented ape'.

Vena's big role was feeding the great pots that had to be boiled at different times of the day. Fuel was plentiful and dry that year and this proved a special blessing.

# CHAPTER 9

# *Matrimony*

The next important news item in the locality was the annoucement of Terna's marriage to Peter. Terna made her plans carefully and tactfully as usual. While she rejoiced in her mother's increased income she was never demanding. She went quietly to the nearest town and purchased soft, rich satin for her wedding dress. Her mother gave her passementerie trimming for it. A white veil, dainty silver shoes and a silver string of white pearls completed the ensemble. People remarked that she looked like a tall lily at the altar. One of Peter's sister's came from overseas to the wedding and arrived on that morning with another sister from Westore. Terna left quietly for the parish church where their grey-haired kindly pastor performed the simple ceremony. General rejoicing and felicitations were on until the married ones left on the three-thirty train to Dublin. The June sun shone after a dark morning just as they left Carfort. Fay was the only bridesmaid. Vena showed genuine pleasure returning to Carfort after the ceremony.

There was a casual friend of Marto's at the wedding. He lived four miles away. Middle-aged, dull and respectable, he fell head, neck and heels in love with Fay. When he discovered that Jock was the right one he became more determined and begged Marto to do his utmost for him and even made him a wonderful offer should he succeed in removing Jock. It failed.

After their honeymoon Peter and Terna visited Westore where Terna found that her in-laws were not of the same disposition as Peter. She found his mother keen and very practical. Terna's fine fairness contrasted strongly with the older woman's dark vitality. The youngest sister, Mara, she admired. Mara had the eyes of a lamb. The district where they lived was a cradle of beauty. The fruit trees, with their rich promise, were good to look at. The family's Hereford cows moved with a matronly gait across verdant pastures.

There was a higher gloss on the grass and the meadows were like yards and yards of water-wave silk. Old trees leaned lovingly towards each other and chirpers hopped happily in them.

Mrs Canning had been a widow for many years then. Most of her family had gone abroad, Mara being the only one at home. After their stay in Westore the newlyweds returned to Carfort and within three weeks Peter had received his transfer to a second class station, Glenmark – forty-five miles away.

When Mister and Mrs Canning were speeding along in the train to their new home in Glenmark Terna's heart swelled at the unfamiliar scenes. Stretches of bog and moor, of sylvan hills, green fields and shady valleys came into view. The season wore a crown of glory. The haze was early. It looked as if it veiled the secrets of a hidden world; the sun hung like a tarnished ring.

'Why don't you sing a song of thanks, you very-much-married old man?' the young wife teased. It was then that her own 'A Te Deum' was born, on a beautiful July afternoon. They were tired and hungry opening the door of the new home. None of the vans carrying their furniture and household effects had arrived so far. So Peter 'phoned the furniture people to send on necessary articles already paid for.

In the meantime they enjoyed a meal in a neighbouring woman's place and then slipped into a church to beg a blessing on their undertakings. The following days were spent arranging things and setting the house in order. Peter had his duties to perform and that meant that much of the fixing came on Terna's shoulders. Then, somehow, after a few months Peter felt congested. The fact that there were poor divisions between the houses at the back accounted for poor privacy. So they moved to Cane Street, Upper, and settled down in harmony. Large beech trees spread their weighty branches opposite the front door. They grew on a neighbour's land.

Glenmark was a place where a whisper could start a story though all the people had much to recommend them in the line of practical abilities and natural decency.

So Terna had to start rearranging and decorating, but she loved the roomy house and the large garden. Peter missed his Sealwell comrades. They were single and light-hearted.

Most of the shops in Glenmark catered for the general run of country people and stocked hard-wearing, coarse tweeds that made up into durable garments. The young wife, however, favoured the finer materials and purchased most of them in the next big town to Glenmark. Peter set out for Dublin at the end of October and returned with a stylish coat with a swagger effect for Terna's first birthday in Glenmark. Terna covered the place with flowers, had an intense love of gladioli and referred to them in a prize-winning poem later:

*In the crimson depth of a sword-shaped flower*
*Is the pierced heart of God ...*

# CHAPTER 10

# *The Unexpected*

Terna and Peter were settling in, though from the beginning she disliked the fact that he had such long hours on duty. She grew accustomed to the new rules. At other times she could be seen wending her way through bogs and country roads receiving impressions for her next poem or story. Unknowingly she made enemies. Some unkind critics soon began to nudge each other as she passed. 'Oh! you'd almost take her to be the lady of the place.' Another: 'And she only a farmer's daughter, a broken-down one at that.' And Terna was so sorry to learn that a person in a responsible position used words to the same effect; and considering that the Carfort uplands were verdant in comparison to the speaker's native place, snipe country.

A kinder critic thought 'that the newcomer appeared to be class of respectable, that her hair was like an angel's and that her walk wasn't bad.'

A few observant idlers gathered in the kitchens of the town at night and discussed the new people. Over their diluted drinks they chatted and chopped until whatever percentage of neat liquor their drinks contained went flat, and one evening, as the happy pair were returning from a long walk, full of vigour, they became unwilling listeners to two good haters near their house: 'A wine-coloured velvet dress walking! The idea of it!' number one laughed. 'Sure,' agreed number two, 'though she might be as wholesome as she's sweet, that one.' The male got away somewhat lighter. 'Easy-going, I'm told, if that's any good all the time.'

To crown it, Peter raised his hat high and Terna smiled a natural smile and passed quietly into the house. Once inside, they peeped out to see a pair of half-mortified women saying goodbye. The Cannings' attitude changed them ... set them wondering ...

It was around that time that the usually genial owner of property in Cane Street, Upper, appeared to be so different. He wore an aggrieved expression over the most trifling incident, and should the sun roll behind a cloud he held his new tenant solely responsible! If the naughty sun rolled out again he complained that they had the use of it before him. The man paced his bedroom floor at night planning playful villainy for people who he thought offended, disliked or disobliged him. Next day was spent half-dozing on a cane chair in his back garden.

When Peter made a new friend in the person of The Very Reverend John Kyle, the unreasonable man created a scene. With a hauteur he dashed into their house and demanded an explanation from his solvent occupiers. 'Let that bloody man stay in his own house! We're all right without him. How well he found you out!' But all to no avail.

The wild one stood six-feet-four in his socks. From that height he looked down on shrivelled man. When pleased, he roared an enquiry for one's health, when angry he was terrible to behold. He glowered, voiced his disapproval incoherently, came a pace nearer, retreated and finally spoke his lines calmly. During those outbursts his wide, black moustache mercifully covered the wrathful foam that escaped from his lip's. He had quasi-notions and believed that he was entitled to hurt if provoked. War was interesting always. After the first sight of him Peter had referred to him as 'Giraffy' on account of his leaning height and long neck. Terna found him an interesting study.

A year and a half after their marriage their daughter, Gay, was born. Terna had everything in readiness to go to a nursing home but she had no time.

Gay was a dimpled bundle with a mop of red-gold hair. The local doctor and nurse termed her a miniature Terna. Gay was their first Christmas box. Terna recovered rapidly and embraced the state of motherhood very sensibly. 'You and I are responsible for this new soul. We have only the loan of Gay,' she impressed on Peter.

When Gay was nine months old her parents left for a vacation in England. Their family were only too anxious to have their first grandchild and niece. The wonderful air of Carfort seemed to be enough to feed the child and she grew strong and rosy there. Peter and Terna sent glowing accounts and gifts to Carfort. They thrilled to their second honeymoon, the voyage and England. They spent three days in Blackpool where they attended a sweet-making exhibition. And from there they proceeded by motor coach to Southport via Preston, a distance of forty miles. The broad level fields around Southport compared well with the pastures in the Irish Midlands and most of the inhabitants there had a cultured outlook. They spent some time in Southport, St Anne's-on-Sea and Liverpool. They also attended a few good shows, seeing Gracie Fields sing, and on their return to Blackpool they saw a beauty Queen crowned and attended a health lecture by a foreign doctor.

> *Oh, landing on that English shore*
> *Where gulls were fed and came for more.*

Terna wrote that later when she recollected in tranquillity in Glenmark. The Fields' charity concert was the highlight of their holiday in Lancashire and Terna's passion for music and song was fully satisfied here. Gracie's rendering of *Roll along, covered wagon, Ave Maria, Sing as you go,* and others, was unforgettable.

On the return journey Terna was very ill so Peter suggested another month for her in Carfort. She revelled in the country emancipation and meeting little Gay again. She praised English cooking and the cleanliness of the homes. She loved the garden city of St Anne's and the floral clock in Blackpool, in Stanley Park. Hundreds of England's people travelled in holiday mood on a beautiful September evening. Terna stood between the evenly-spaced trees to drink in the beauty of the place and the deep peace. Hovering pleasure planes could be seen and heard. The dappled haze wrapped the city and obscured the sun, then thunder howled with vengeance and lightning flashes appeared like splinters from the hidden sun. Inside a brightly-lit church then Terna prayed: 'Oh, God! bless this England and bring it to yourself again!'

At the end of their month in Carfort Peter collected Terna and Gay. The Brantons missed both of their visitors. Gay had filled their lives. They would miss the turn of her small head, her smile and her laughing eyes.

During her stay in Carfort Terna saw two things that troubled her: her mother's anaemic pallor and the usually erect Will's unhealthy-looking stoop. The latter's ear was mastoid and he complained of pains in his back. He had, altogether, a really dejected air.

## CHAPTER II

# *Sadness and Joy*

The Canning family were progressing favourably in Glenmark. Each day was better than the other. Their daughter toddled and laughed most of her waking hours and then would sink into a healthy sleep when bedtime came.

They made a point to be kindly disposed towards their immediate neighbours from the first. Time was important to the family and Terna loved the moment when she could pen a few verses in solitude. With the precious addition to her and Peter every minute was filled, so solitude was a luxury. Both husband and wife were into the official routine by then and time was pleasantly passed between daily Mass and interesting engagements socially. That year they had planned to take Gay with them on Peter's leave in a month or so. But what they proposed was abruptly changed by a letter from Carfort stating that Will was seriously ill and being removed to hospital with meningitis. Terna was more shocked than surprised. After her brother, her next thought was for her mother who had had her share of sadness already, looking at fine, old Carfort in reduced circumstances.

She sat down at once and rushed a consoling letter to her family and offered the best help of all pending her departure, spiritual hope. Nevertheless, religious trust failed to work a miracle. No human aid could spare Will. After three operations in a few hours in Sir Patrick Dunn's Hospital in Dublin he passed away with a smile on his lips and was buried in the family grave in Kilcross. Terna travelled to Dublin with her sisters and they were told in the hospital by a nurse that Will's last words were that 'Dad would miss him at the beet.' Vena fell silent in grief while Fay wept openly and Terna saw herself back in his little pink room in Carfort praying for him as she so often did before! Many young people of his own age who had enjoyed his singing and music, followed his remains and gathered round the headstone that had been erected years before by his late grandfather, a man of worth. Will's mother carried her new cross with dignity but knew the pain of being deprived of son and constant solace.

Being back on such a painful errand in Carfort changed everything for the Cannings. Instead of a long holiday elsewhere, they stayed to comfort and console the bereaved ones, for the silence and emptiness that follows death remained for several months. Dick went around the fields with his pipe dangling from his lips while he forgot to pull on it, and he walked a while, then stood and thought a while, pulled once on his pipe and made a sorry sight without mentioning his inexpressible sorrow to anybody.

So later, at the call of duty, Terna and Gay arrived back in Cane Street, the young mother battling bravely for her parents' sake. When the Carfort letters arrived she read loneliness and heartbreak between their lines. Dick was to learn slowly to bury his grief in an abyss of resignation and she would wean herself from the oft-recurring thought of Will's death.

Then one morning another epistle cheered them. Peter's wealthy brothers were coming home to Ireland from the States. They would enliven the whole circle and give it something to talk about. Even Gay guessed that there was something forthcoming for she gurgled and smiled more in her playpen with her eyes on Terna.

So in a few days a massive, grey car glided slowly to the front door. Peter was absent. Terna ran to meet the visitors for she instantly recognised Michael and Ray out of Peter. Michael was, perhaps, the most readily genial and talkative. The brothers had picked up Mara and a friend in Westore. The girls were delighted to accompany them to Peter's. As they all turned towards the house Peter saw them and jumped off his bicycle to join them. The joy of meeting his long-absent brothers was great, indeed. The visitors stayed the best part of a week and then sprang a surprise on the Carfort in-laws, much to the latter's delight. Brantons was their home for a short time ... with the arrangement that they were to come back when they liked after ...

Terna's married life at this stage amounted to dull routine, so Michael's surprise visits to Glenmark made for variety. In her spare time she committed her thoughts to paper, though even this showed that the *trend* of thought was often broken in the follow-up required, for Will's death was a constant ache when she was alone. Peter noticed this and its effect on her, so he suggested a trip to the States with his brothers for her and Gay. Impossible, for she was expecting another addition to the family on or around Gay's third birthday. It was a boy with red-gold hair like Gay's, who was christened Vane. Peter was very proud of his son and preferred to call his hair chestnut when he lay asleep in the sun. He was proud of his daughter also and still prouder of Terna.

At home in Brantons everything was at a standstill. The new hope that the family knew through poor Will's excellent endeavours to set Carfort on its feet again was gone forever. The same buyer was still active and Dick, Honoria, Vena and Marto lived from day to day, while Honoria was accepting things that she could not change. She was nearly seventy years old then. Marto was disinclined to settle in marriage. The very thought repelled him. He took a scrappy interest in things since his brother died even though his father had signed his place over to him. Terna explained that perhaps Marto felt that he was not cut out for managing a big farm. She disapproved so strongly that Dick regretted handing over his property.

Fay and Jock were still all in all and waiting to name the day when Jay announced his intention to marry. A pale, kindly-faced girl with a slow gait, good humour and a nice dowry attracted his notice and eventually won his heart. The Cannings could not attend the wedding for some official reason. Seven sturdy children came to their prosperous home in Cratton. Next to her duties Terna occupied herself with writing, and sometimes there were acceptance slips with small cheques. Some six months later when visiting in Cratton she informed them that there was another little Canning on the way, and that it would be a girl with golden hair and would be a leader. Terna was correct to the letter.

Blitz was born during a heat-wave and remained delicate for some years until her mother brought her to the Shrine of Our Lady of Knock in County Mayo to cure her of her indisposition. And so she did. Blitz was a clever child. After her birth her mother had constant pain and weakness in her back. She slept very badly at night for the new baby was restless and noisy and could not hold her food. Once wakened, Terna could not settle down again. She often longed to relax on the wide moors of Carfort, joining the Common, with the patient mother who lived there.

Oh, happy, happy days of carefree childhood! Terna often looked at her children and wondered if they were better off than she had been, leading urbanised lives. She had a strong, abiding faith in the Supreme Creator's Plan. Her belief was simple and sure in those days. So this built-in belief left her ready for all vicissitudes. She was forced to keep a helper now as work seemed an effort. A nice, agreeable girl came to live in, and the children soon looked on her as a pal.

One night Terna went upstairs. On the landing she said to Madge: 'Somehow I feel that Vane is going to fall ill.' Madge cheered her saying that it was just being run down and the extra responsibility that made her apprehensive. The transformation in the young mother was touching while it lasted but more touching when it evaporated a week after when Vane was rushed to a hospital for an urgent operation for a perforated appendix. While Vane was fighting peritonitis Terna was struggling to keep up her courage and Peter travelled to the hospital every day. Terna was not equal to this, so she rang regularly. Vane was lucky to have had a very skilful doctor with much practice and very well known in his field. And good-natured Fay came to help her over her troubles and shared the joy of of setting out to the hospital some weeks later to take poor, wasted Vane home. Then Terna sped in spirit to the little pink room to thank God for His Providence. Vane was rolled in a heavy blanket and put to bed just that way immediately the parents and Fay returned. Tender care soon brought colour to his cheeks again and he conversed with everybody.

Just when things were humming again in Cane Street and the little ex-patient in the capable hands of Madge, Peter's then arthritic mother was called away rather suddenly. The Cannings attended the obsequies. Terna had become a consolatrix to all by now and the right words came easily to her. Her words relieved Mara who was now married with two children. Her husband was a well-off widower, a professional farmer with one child. Peter missed his mother deeply and found it hard to concentrate on his work for months.

The following twelve months proved to be quite uneventful. The humdrum life of Glenmark went on and Terna had made a new friend. Funnily enough, the friend's name was Kathleen Canning, though no relation. Those two had much in common and in time Terna became a frequent visitor in her friend's house. She always had that home-from-home feeling there. Kathleen was very level-headed and sensible, much easier to get on with than the tense and emotional type. She had three brothers, the eldest a zealous, religious kind, and the others more of the saturnine.

The three young Cannings thrived well and were very bright and alert, though Blitz had fairly indifferent health. Gay attended the local national school and had already started music in the town. Her teacher was young and had a diploma, and Gay liked her.

Terna was gardening a while later when Peter handed her a letter in familiar handwriting. It held the news that Marto had signed over his place to Vena and that she was preparing to get married. Everything seemed rushed and unreal, though within a fortnight she had an invitation to the wedding in her hand. Two lines of her verse ran through her head:

> *Sadness and joy in turns call*
> *And seeds from joy forever fall.*

The Cannings were delighted that Carfort was on its feet again. The new manager seemed to have good business abilities. Vena was some years older than Terna. The change was beneficial. Soon Carfort's acres were grazed to the roots by mixed breeds of cattle. Flocks of white sheep nursed tender lambs in the fields and new horses whinnied musically at each other. The poultry farming proved to be an outstanding success though Vena's husband, Eddy, believed in more and more stock and less tillage. The huge common, in its own way, was a big advantage for grazing was available at a nominal rent.

Jay had received the gift of a daughter by this time. People said that she was a born Branton, but Jay's parents would not agree. The parents moved around more by then, staying for weeks with Terna and for shorter periods with Jay in Cratton. All the marrieds sought Honoria's advice and hated to see her leave. Terna loved making surprise presents to her mother. The latter suffered from acute pains and was generally washy. Terna insisted that she should lie down every day after lunch. This worked until her mother returned to Carfort where she could never find a minute to rest.

Fay's marriage to Jock followed Vena's marriage quickly. More presents when Peter's wife and Gay set off and enjoyed meeting old and new friends. She brought a set of fine china to Fay. The set had landscape designs all over it. Carfort had emptied quickly, and Fay and Jock were rightly blessed as Jock's mother was the essence of commonsense and goodness to them. But she did not live long enough to enjoy her first grandchild – a boy.

The months flew by. Terna's health had improved, for her very will to be well helped her along. Short manuscripts were piling up and she had been publishing verse occasionally in both home and overseas editions. She had breakfast cooked and school preparations made before 9.30 each morning. Kitchen and rooms were then turned out, baking at 10.30 and shopping at 11.00. This method gave her a chance of an hour's writing before lunch and three hours after – though Madge was indispensable.

Then Peter received an order to leave on temporary transfer to another quarter. Though busier, Terna succeeded in getting to bed at night before 10.30, and the outside world saw very little of her until he returned. Gay guessed how she felt and grew brighter and more obliging in the house. Madge appreciated it. And when Peter eventually returned there followed a long rest for the mother and the children and a few months after that the Cannings' fourth and last child was born. Baby Jay was the only dark haired child in the family. He had his father's colouring and bone structure and his mother wrote later:

> *When he is wrapt in angel's sleep*
> *I sometimes peep into his cot,*
> *And suddenly feel ill at ease,*
> *What would I do if he were not?*

The anxiety expressed in the above lines was heightened for Terna by the arrival of a telegram one afternoon that her mother was sinking fast. She had rapid diabetes, and despite the best medical care, she failed to respond or rally. The family had kept the news from Terna first, thinking it better that way. For once in her life she did not go in spirit to the little, pink room of happy memory and ask a cure, but like her mother, calmly hoped to accept what she could not change. She hardly waited to dress until she was at her mother's side. 'I am dying, Terna!' her mother said sadly. Weakly as she was, the dying woman made an effort to get on her elbow to kiss her daughter but Terna eased her back on the pillow and spoke of heavenly things. While the terrible pain of loneliness touched her own heart she tried to cast that fact aside to help and prepare her mother. Imagine the wonder in that home when Terna declared that the dying woman would linger for three weeks. And up to the last she had her presence of mind. The fact that Carfort was prospering served to heighten her passing, and the sight of her children around her at her last moments made her happier still. 'Terna!' she whispered, 'I'll be with Will.'

Poor Marto was the weakest in their new sorrow. Perhaps the knowledge that he had pained his mother by causing the name to be changed had given him qualms of conscience. Vena and her husband, Tim, who never forgot Terna's words, hardly left the room where she lay while Terna and Fay came and went regularly.

At the end of the third week on a fine Saturday morning on the ninth of October, Mrs Branton passed away while she uttered the words: 'I – will – be – with – Will.' She used Dick's name a few times. She was buried in the Kilcross grave where many grasses and a few flowers waved lightly in the breezes. And as the thud of the clay sounded on her coffin a tall, dark-eyed bachelor made his way through the crowd to hold Terna's hands in sympathy. There and then was she stricken at the aged appearance of her husband's former rival ... he had an empty heart ... an empty life.

When a mother dies the foundation of a family is gone. If the children disperse it is usual for them to lose nature for the old home. The mother's vacant chair speaks volumes; her treasured bequests bring tears; the way she liked to do things, how she understood.

When Dick asked Terna to have her mother's wedding ring, she refused. Her reason for not accepting it was characteristic: 'If I wear it, it will make me cry; if I have her prayer book it will make me pray for her.' She wanted her departed mother to have the best end of the arrangement. Her philosophical mind was still in gear. Dick's powers of endurance stood to him then, but he seldom spoke. Though still erect and handsome, his hair was white. One could imagine that the sole ambition left to him was to die. But the family rallied round and kept him interested in everything and everybody from his new granddaughter born much later, who was just an edition of her Southern father. All threw themselves into their work and recreation, the growing families calling for extra planning and attention.

Peter gave Terna the sobriquet of 'the human printing press'. All her longhand was shorthand, so swiftly did she write. More than once a publisher looked interested; more often she found his terms unreasonable.

Dick threw himself into his new pastime, too. He spent hours on the Common with his gun. Absence from the house eased the parting.

But after five and a half months of mourning he said goodbye to life and welcomed *death*. He had gone, to find again the bright, guiding star of his life that he had lost a while.

Terna wrote on the first anniversary of her mother's death:

> *The holy, little cemetery*
> *Below the Kilcross church*
> *Shelters souls who used to be*
> *My earthly parents first.*

CHAPTER 12

# *Happy Responsibilities*

Peter and Terna had but one objective in view — the upbringing of their four children. Both of them worked as one for the following years. Terna learned that work was the best antidote to grief, and she found happiness in simple things from day to day. She lived by the clock. Her creative work proved to be a medium of mental travel for her. And after the round of births, marriages and deaths, things and people in and around Glenmark became interesting; for instance, when she paid a visit to the butcher, baker or draper. The cost of living was sky-high and increased expenditure gave her a real opening to show her capability to balance the family budget. Under no circumstances did she want Peter and herself to *owe* rather than *own* money.

And luckily at this juncture Peter's wealthiest brother, Michael, used to send very good financial advice when least expected. Peter had heavy insurances but no arrears. Both valued the privilege of independence.

Some experiences amused Terna, but they were not all that funny. Such as the day she shopped outside Glenmark, when she entered a butcher's premises with a large banknote in her hand. The beefy butcher's wrinkled face beamed at the sight of the note and set about sawing the T-Bone steaks that she had not called for yet. Once after that on a day off, when she called for the family joint and had the amount and the cost entered in his books, just for the time being, he barely muttered a churlish 'thanks' and handed her the parcel with averted face. Another with whom she dealt must have come to the conclusion that she was one to overlook things easily and graciously. Once Terna read out her list and withdrew to change a cheque in a bank. She had the list of the items in her handbag. When she called back to pay and get the receipt she found that harmless extras had been added here and there. She coolly presented the list and had his mistake, as she tactfully put it, corrected.

On another occasion, nearer home, an honest assistant passed on what he described as delightfully crunchy buns in a closed paper packet. On arrival home Terna examined the contents to discover that the crunchies were ancient, plain buns that would test the tusks of an elephant to break them. She returned the packet with a polite reminder that the buns were not, in fact, crunchies, and would he kindly send her one of his fresh loaves. She had saved his face. The same day a wizened old age pensioner said to her: 'They would not care if wan was dead, only to get wan's funeral expenses.'

Next, Michael Canning arrived by plane in Ireland and later to Glenmark. His Glenmark relatives had yet to taste of the fairy god-father kindness of that much-travelled gentleman. As before, Peter was absent when he arrived. Terna and the children were playing when he drove in his Packard to the place and the young people climbed into his car with greetings and exciting questions with hand-shakes. Terna had to help him to get into the house. Then she began to relate all the items of interest in Glenmark and their circle. The children had to take their turns when he brought them out during his three-month stay in Ireland. Their mother would not have it otherwise and left nothing undone to make his holiday a happy one. She looked on his last gift – a golden Rosary beads – as a precious heirloom. He flew back home when the glory that is Autumn showed in Glenmark. She and Peter saw most of Ireland with him.

After his departure Terna wrote a story for a competition but felt that her chances of getting a prize were slender. Competition was keen with older writers competing. She was pleasantly surprised when she won a small prize.

Peter received a considerable increase in salary when he was just despairing of getting any. They were on a better footing then. On top of Michael's visit Peter had been planning a vacation in Westore for the whole family. Terna had everything in preparation by the time his leave started. Westore was all that is said and written about it. That time the harvest gold was a sight. Stooks and stacks stood in mellow richness in yard and field all over the county of Westmeath. Some tillage fields had produced two crops in the year. The land there was very rich and the stretches of roads with giant, overhanging trees provided striking scenery for the camera. As far as Terna was concerned, she was rather on her own, for the women she had met there before had gone away. Even so, the children enjoyed themselves and looked tanned after the air and sun when they arrived home in Glenmark.

The other members of the Brantons prospered and expanded, Marto enjoying single bliss and still in Carfort where his advice and guidance were valued. It was well known that two ladies openly proposed marriage to him and that he commented later: 'Wouldn't you wonder that they didn't wait until *I* asked *them*? I suppose they knew that I never would.'

The eldest, married sister of Peter's family made a six weeks' visit some weeks after the Westore vacation. She resembled Michael but lacked his engaging personality. She had no family and found it difficult to team up with those bouncing nieces and nephews. Their sudden, impish pranks upset her habitual quiet. So she curtailed her visit and moved among her older relatives staying only a short time in each place. The young Cannings found their elderly, handsome aunt too precise and exacting, and she, in turn, failed to understand them.

When Blitz unwittingly asked her if she were as rich as Uncle Michael, her aunt asked her 'if she would prefer a very rich uncle to a not-so-rich aunt.' Blitz was too pert for her. Before Aunt Alice left Vane and Gay stayed out late with friends after the cinema and their aunt asked Terna if the children were put to bed so early every other night! She was under the impression that they had been in bed since 7.45. Terna replied vaguely and indistinctly, and was delighted when her sister-in-law decided to retire before the children flung themselves in the front door. They, in turn, felt as if some tiresome restriction had been removed when they had the living room to themselves. Slim-legged Gay wakened Blitz to fit the beautiful frocks from the States. Pale blue, mauve, pink and green were the predominating colours on them. The green mixtures looked best on the two little blondes, while Vane and Jay sported their Jack Tar suits with sailor collars. Even Peter thrilled over a grey lumber jacket while Terna fitted spotted silks and crepe-de-chines.

The most expensive garment among Gay's new wardrobe was a coat of summer ermine. Terna wondered if the child were too young to appreciate it and wished that the kind aunt had delayed its giving.

Terna gave her new shoes to go with it such as the magically-changed Cinderella could wear.

One evening when Terna had sent the children to gather mushrooms that had appeared later than usual, a light knock on the door brought her flying to open it. Kathleen Canning had come to invite her to her wedding. Terna could not travel as Peter was engaged on a job that called for long journeys. So she mailed another gift. Kathleen married a farmer about twice her age and died young. Terna's old clerical friend was then an invalid and with all her pressing duties she made time to visit and console him. And when she failed to do so, she sent him the choicest blooms in her garden. This friend charmed her with his easy wit and learning, and many were the laughs that passed between them. Terna told him that he had a twinkle in his eye like an Irish leprechaun before he stole the crock of gold. Her friend died as the Angelus rang in Glenmark on a March evening. He had predicted an hour before that he would go then, and his nurses waited to see it happen.

# CHAPTER 13

# Pleasure and Pain

The secluded lanes and byways around the town of Glenmark afforded
the perfect settings for poet and artist. A skilful landscape painter had
ample material for his canvas in this partly-wooded district of many
run-lets and rivulets. The one large river in the place boasted a few
graceful, white swans. Terna had become friendly with those
birds and fed them from the river banks. At sight of her the birds
approached, but when their cygnets appeared, the older birds resented
her presence.

With the children and the elderly Madge, Terna used to pack a
picnic basket and stay for hours in the open. They took dozens of
pictures with the Glenmark scenery in the background. One of the
pictures showed Blitz in a playsuit with wind-blown hair, eating an
apple and evidently enjoying it. A smooth field dotted with white
sheep, some of them under low ash trees, made a delightful feature.
Lots of these snaps were sent to the married members of both families.

A young lady who held a position of trust in Glenmark was a
frequent guest of the Cannings. This lady had spent a few years in a
convent and the aura of religious discipline still hung about her. The
friendship lasted for many years until the ex-nun decided to become
the wife of a farmer with a large tract of land. In this case a doctor
warned her not to attempt pregnancy the second time, but she ignored
what he advised and was buried three years after her marriage, her
husband marrying his cousin some eighteen months later.

Suddenly the wanderlust seized Terna and she left her family in the
efficient Madge's care and set off on a cycling tour, of all things! She
was eager to gather material for a new story and all her auditory and

visual powers were fully exercised. She packed a folding wardrobe and had it forwarded to the address of an old school friend in whose house she would be a welcome, though uninvited, guest. She planned to cycle the hundred miles and make the return by train. She moved slowly at first, barely hiding the girlish gleam of exhilaration in her eyes. The country colours were dingy compared with the soft pink of clouds, but the dinginess was not depressing, for it reminded her of the inevitable and natural process of decay.

As she went along she noticed the roadsides flanked by laburnum gone out of flower. Instead of the yellow blooms only poisonous pods remained. She thought of Westore, that fertile parcel in the east with its lustrous scenes. Now and then she dismounted and chatted to strangers, homely ones, so that she could listen to their dialect and the accents peculiar to their different regions. She found them all pleasing and natural.

Then she helped herself to the goodies that Madge had provided, sitting by a well near the road with careless ease. A farmer came along carrying a bucket of milk and enquired if she cared for some. She smiled her pleasure and accepted the milk gratefully. When the man had gone she spent a half hour in deep thought, then cast a glance in the direction of the spotless cottage from which he had emerged. There were a few children at play, with skin like milk and cheeks like the early roses in her Cane Street garden. Loathe to leave, she counted the seconds of her solitude and penned lines mentally so that she would not lose the impressions that she was receiving at every turn. Her eyes fell on an expanse of water as still as bulb light until a swarm of coloured flies stirred it and the sun of noon created a diorama from their colours. The long puffs of contented cattle and the calls of grown-up lambs reached her. From afar off, the rumbling of carts drawn by heavy horses, conjured up activities in Carfort and hot tears filled her eyes slowly.

Mounting her bicycle again she was soon invisible to the good cottage folk. Instantly her humour changed from sad remembering to her former exhilaration.

The afternoon changed, darkened, but suddenly the circle of the sun shone again like a great spotlight on the land. At a turning of the wide road a grey-haired woman and a girl of eight or so appeared. The woman saluted her friendlily and the girl asked what she was doing there. Terna told her that she was running away from home.

'I don't believe you,' the youngster said. 'Why have you your plaits twisted all over your head?'

'Because my mother liked this fashion,' she was told, and then the woman beckoned to her not to interrogate any longer and she blushed and grew silent.

'Never mind, dear!' Terna said. 'Intelligent questions are always interesting.' The girl was pleased and laughed happily, so Terna raised her camera and caught another snapshot for her collection. Then she said good-bye.

The next building was a small, spotless church. To her delight there was a service on for a young person who died some months before. The service had been requested by a friend. The peace, prayers and lights suited her. She gave thanks for the atmosphere before she left and recommended Peter and all to the care of God.

It was evening when she landed in a smallish village. She was feeling tired and walked through it. She heard light laughs from a doorway, a dirty opening, and she wondered if they, too, noticed her plaits in the evening light, or if the gigglers had been educated in the common art of sniggering ridicule. She ordered a mineral and was seized with longing to get out of the place.

Once more on her bicycle, the soft shadows of the early night closed in slowly around her. Other village noises fell. The rattle of cans, the soft lowing of mother cows, the wheezy whispers of sleepy hens as they remained close in downy warmth, noisy flights of crows and the late twitters of tiny birds in bushes. A lonely gull shrieked and she supposed that it was far away from home like herself. She experienced a passing mood of loneliness and incompleteness. Oh! the utterly indescribable joy of being alone – alone with the new night on its course. From being engrossed in the mystery of darkness and depth where wonder held the mastery, she slid back again to earth and to the bicycle at her feet that held her picnic basket, tiny flask and camera. She saw the whole canvas of her life studded with the stars of her desires and ambitions and she wished to succeed or fail on her own merits. Her untiring efforts to achieve certain goals appeared like wonderful pulleys drawing her along, ever onwards and upwards to those goals. Maybe it was an uplifting, religious notion only.

Had she not known difficulties and problems she would never have climbed those splendid ladders of gold that she had just seen before her mental vision, sheer joy of wakening up from a dream that was to come true, following hope. In rapt reasoning, she set off again on a road that was now only the width of the light thrown on it from her lamp.

Her eyes were heavy as she dismounted to look for accommodation. She thought of the house in Cane Street, with soft radio music, Peter's cautious stepping around the homely kitchen, Gay's singing with the radio, and Blitz teasing poor, patient Vane. And Madge's vigilance and careful collection of letters in her absence. At heart, the traveller would have preferred to have slept near a haycock, though unseemly. Away from Glenmark noises and passing traffic and the odd, nervous tension that arises in town houses in very warm weather. The head-aches, late retiring and broken sleep, the moments that even the scents of her many flowers through the open window could not soothe away.

She braced herself for the job before her on a trackless way. She left her bicycle by a railing and peered through the windows of a row of brightly lit houses that were all painted cream. If the interior were half as clean as the exterior she would be satisfied to pass the night in one of them. One of the inmates noticed her and came forward. She wore a snowy white overall and her hair appeared to be sprinkled with stardust.

Terna approached courteously and enquired if she belonged to the house. The girl informed her that she did and readily understood what the matter was. She slipped into the kitchen for a minute and was back directly saying that her mother would manage to put her up and showed her her room. Terna beamed her thanks and passed quietly upstairs. She turned back the embroidered cover and sat on the bed. A soft knock on the door roused her. She opened it promptly to the neat girl's mother with a glass of fresh milk and biscuits. The woman spoke first. The plain words had feeling in them. 'As it is a little late, Miss! I wouldn't be givin' ya somethin' stodgy so as to keep ya awake all night.' She left the tray and departed, and soon Terna's tired body sank into a sleep that was to last as long as the laws of nature allowed.

She was as fresh as the first yellow flags growing in the marshes of Carfort the next morning. With outstretched hands she smiled at the thought of another day in the open. 'On the road to anywhere,' she half said, half sang as she dressed and felt glad that she had sent on her holiday outfit already. She inhaled the fragrance of late shrubs through the window. They had a heavy, mingled scent. Then she tidied around and went down to breakfast after her toilet, taking the tray with her. Her bedroom was drab next to the dining room, small though it was. A cloth with blue motifs of bluebirds covered the mirror-like table. The napkins had similar motifs. Crisp rashers, eggs and country bread made the menu, and after the long intakes of air on the day before she was able to do justice to the meal. Then she settled her account and rose to go.

The road was hilly. A soft wind blew at that early hour and the sun was already climbing the sky. The sun threw shafts of gold over dark streams making them look darker. A waterfall in the distance filled the morning with swishing notes. A bell toiled and a mill wheel slowly revolved into action. When she passed a closed church she paused to leave her soul at the altar but her heart she kept in the cavity of her thorax to assist her to cover the miles ahead under a peaceful sky. As she moved off she asked herself why there were only half a dozen people waiting at the church for admission when the local cinema would have to provide extra seats that night for shallow entertainment.

She closed her eyes behind her sunglasses with a reflective laugh at the comparison.

# CHAPTER 14

# *Great Joys*

Alone with the wonderful vistas, Terna could have sung with the hedge warblers but she preferred to listen. Their trilling seemed to follow her. It was 11.30 a.m. Reaching a small newsagent's she bought a paper and sitting later on a mossy knoll she scanned its headlines. 'Oh, dear!' she thought. 'It is war and more war for this lovely world! And the value of a human being!' She jotted down on the back of an envelope:

*The Heavens see red, so red they could ignite ...*
*That Right is ousted by so much wrong!*

When she folded the envelope she looked up and saw a few black and white birds flying past. Large and small vehicles appeared. Some drivers blew their horns, so that she had plenty of time to watch and to regulate her speed at the sharp bends of the road.

Feeling hungry then she ordered some solid food in a store and was addressed as 'Miss' again. Wondering if a pleasant, ruddy-faced country man should accept her newspaper she was not surprised when he did, and neither was she when he thanked her profusely, saying that if he had met her earlier he would have been spared a whole hour for his farm work – for he had come to buy one. The man offered to pay for her refreshments but she declined to accept his kind offer.

Terna expected to reach her destination that evening. After helping herself to the food she rang Peter to reassure herself that all was well. The noon sun was blotted out by a few hardy showers in succession so she ran to the shelter of a close hedge. When the clouds dispersed and the rain ceased, she was about to set out joyously again when her eyes fell on a large cluster of clovers – about four dozen of four- and five-leafed ones. Though she never listened to superstition, she stooped and plucked those plants of supposed good omen and placed them in her basket. And recalled that once before she unaccountably bent and plucked a five-leafed clover from her father-in-law's grave in Westore.

A clear sun was at its zenith in the blue by this time. People were busy on either side of the road. Women wearing headsquares leaned over spades with their menfolk. Twins in a pram close by voiced their grievances but their mothers were too busy to heed them. Terna's motherly administrations such as offering the twins a piece of biscuit, were discouraged by their father. 'Never mind them, Miss! That's their way of gettin' what they want. Take no notice, not a darn bit ... Let them bawl!'

As she swung into the open again she strained every muscle to make up for delays. Then she remembered that it was Blitz's birthday and mailed her a gift from the nearest Post Office as well as a card with the words: 'God bless you on your birthday', written inside a ring of coloured flowers.

Sometimes as she sped along she would slow down to ensure that the dark young man's encased medal had not fallen from its chain round her neck. She grew hungry later and ordered lunch in a crowded hotel, deciding to have a light meal later. Before she partook of her repast she sank into a hot bath to refresh herself. This did away with the necessity of having one in her friend's house. Then as she resumed her journey within an hour, feeling Terna Branton of Carfort all over again, every aspect of life in her home in Cane Street floated in and out of her mind.

Contentment is a crown of solid gold. She was glad she had decided on the cycling tour and she planned to stay out of doors most of the time for its duration, for she had promised Gay dozens of snaps for her album. She also hoped to purchase drapery for all.

As she proceeded, a funeral procession moved slowly towards a graveyard and she learned how detached and casual an onlooker can be when someone else's little stream of life has ebbed away to be swallowed in an invisible tide. Her own comment:

*Dead to earth's worst, alive to Heaven's best.*

The poignant sight of mourners stood out in sharp contrast to the top-of-the-world look of shoppers.

There was an impressive plantation in the distance and here she grew busy with her camera. Just by chance she requested a strange young man if he should oblige by showing her the direction of the chief places of interest in the surrounding district and leading off from the plantation. The helper agreed readily. She judged by his demeanour that he was not in a regular job. She posed for holiday-look pictures to amuse her family; the sights and landmarks, and finally a snap of her friend, and that understood to be posted on. After so much activity in the open her tourist's face was blood-red for her holiday frocks allowed the noon sun full rein for the two days.

Shortly after saying a grateful goodbye to the fellow she had occasion to dismount to rearrange the basket. At that point a splay-mouthed itinerant appeared on the scene. He was good-humoured with a deep, brown skin, and she instantly labelled him Sétanta. The pleasant creature said earnestly: 'Ah, then now, Miss, what would yer be thinkin' of, stayin' out under the broilin' hate on yer bare head?' She explained that she could endure the heat outside much better than when confined to a hot house.

'And glory be, Miss, suppose you dhrop down and ye travellin' alone, an' ye roasted.' He moved nearer, genuinely put out.

'Ah,' she answered, 'there is always someone about and I am not so tender as you think. I shall never see thirty again.'

He broke into a laugh of disbelief. 'Go away with yourself! Isn't it in top form y'are for jokin' this evenin? Ah! me poor toes are stickin' to aich uther, God help me! 'Tisn't aisy workin' with farmers. I wish I was a lad with time on me hands and a camera an' all to sling up on me.'

At that moment Terna promptly clicked the last number to go on the camera. They agreed that he should have his picture at a *poste restante* address later.

The warm evening was turning to a cooler night when she found herself within a distance of fifteen miles of her friend's house. Already she could recognise the old scenes and the boundaries of the different places, most of which had their share of cushy new houses not lacking amenities. Most of the places that she passed had only an acre of land and some others were sited on eight or ten acres. In her friend's area there were larger houses and some recently-erected bungalows. Then fatigue set in from her mounting and dismounting so often, so she decided to shorten her journey by halting a passing bus, thereby arriving at 9.30 p.m.

The Kay of other days received her with a motherly kindness, nor would she listen to her apologising for her late arrival. Kay pushed the dusty Raleigh bicycle into safety and relieved her visitor of her load. The house was in apple-pie order. All her grown-up family were married or fixed in jobs. Referring to Terna's apology, the warm hostess said: 'Relatives we have always with us but distant friends seldom.'

The two chatted until the country dawn coloured the rim of the horizon and streaked the flat places with its ancient artistry. Then, try as they would, the friends found it impossible to continue as they were, and retired. Both Terna's brain and bones were fagged and she rose very late next day, feeling very stiff. Everything was in readiness when she descended in the afternoon. Kay had been up and busy since an early hour.

By the late afternoon they were ready for an outing in the nearest provincial town. Terna was relieved that a cool breeze had come to stay. She had already forwarded a parcel of useful things and confectionery to her friend there and Kay loved them. The visitor chose her other gifts carefully, considering the age and taste of each recipient. Her sons valued guns and mechanical things; Blitz, wearables both for her dolls and herself; and even though past the age for toys Gay valued the soft, cuddly animals still. Peter, of course, preferred a plain silk tie or shirt.

With one moment more enjoyable than the other, during which Kay's magnetic personality and entertaining manner never gave her a time to think, the visitor hardly realized that there was a week of her stay passed.

Certain friends of Kay invited them out and pressed them to call later. But even though Terna was gratefully impressed, deep down she missed a little communing with the receptive plains and spaces that stretched away from the house. She counted on this.

The next evening was ideal for her purpose. Kay had to make a phone call, so she directed her guest to amuse herself as best she could until she returned. At once Terna donned a pink and white frock that Peter's eldest sister had given her. The frock was of a heavier material than her other ones and suited her to perfection. Then grabbing her newly-loaded camera, she swept off to the farthest fields of the farm that was so well laid out and fenced. She chose a corner of a triangular field to work from and watched the healthy stock fill themselves with the new, sweet grass, then breathe hard with swinging heads while their tongues manipulated the mouthfuls before they chewed and swallowed them. Next the animals were snapped at different angles, groups of settled sheep resenting her presence off and on.

A shower that threatened passed off and she entered another field that reminded her of one in Carfort where she used to play and help clean a well with a layer of spawn and slimy green on it. The Carfort place was known as Bolly. The remains of a house with stone walls surrounds were there, possibly from the first generation of Brantons.

She checked her reminiscing to compose two lines of a pastoral:

> Ovine eyes start on seeing me,
> Softer in their timidity.

The evening was like a balm out there in the silent fields. She had a jealous preoccupation with and appreciation of the aesthetic pressure she enjoyed and that she found so satisfying. It seemed that the strange pastures were yielding up the rare and the beautiful, twins to harmonize with her more and more. Or was it sheep when they inspired the first lines of a pastoral that she hoped to finish in Glenmark? She stayed on a little while letting it all sink in for future snatches of happiness. Then she changed into Terna, the woman landing back to earth after soaring so far in her kind of reality. She was back before Kay came with all the local news and developments. In all she spent ten days with Kay – days that entirely coloured her life.

# CHAPTER 15

# *Return*

When Terna arrived in Glenmark she found everybody and everything exactly as she left them, only the children were paler. All items of interest were discussed and nobody had sad news. After an appetising meal Madge brought her her correspondence that had piled up and she perused it all. In a few hours she felt like a spoke in a wheel, she was so fixed and adjusted once again.

Her next outdoor activity was in the flower and vegetable garden. Flowers held a constant fascination for her from the earliest bloom to the latest dahlia and weeds were never allowed to become invasive. Peter shared her love of the hellebore and looked on it as a leader with its alabaster smoothness in all weathers. After a day among the flowers, stooping and straightening, thinking, transplanting, debudding and dead-heading, Terna once inhaled a mixed bunch of carnations and was gripped by a certain afflatus which resulted in her composing a hemistich:

*Heads sunned to blooming.*

Passing a mirror that day she noticed that the sunburn of a week before was still in the process of peeling. She recalled the splay-mouthed speaker's concern for her when Madge suggested a soothing ointment of some sort.

Peter's holidays were now due and Terna advised a long rest by the sea after so many late patrols, but like herself, he had his plans and she loved to see him carry them out. He decided on Carfort with the children where there were two new cousins to meet. Madge and Terna worked hard in preparation and there was a constant rush until the father and young people finally departed.

With the house in order once more, Terna planned little dishes that were different for the menu so that Madge would have a chance to get out more often to visit her people and friends. Madge appreciated the gesture and fell in with the suggestion, saying that it would serve as a kind of holiday for the time being. It suited both of them and Terna would have the quiet required for looking into the impressions and ideas of the time she had spent away.

But the joyous poring was to be disturbed. One day just as Madge was about to leave, a small ramshackle car with two unshaven occupants pulled up. After a glance at them the girl said nervously that she would rather if the boss were home. Terna went to the door with an enquiring look. One of the men was well known to her. She stood by the open door and Madge came to her side. Then the two men stepped smartly inside without being invited and the tougher one, known locally as Scundy, who had the habit of borrowing rather than buying, blurted out: 'Will ya gie me me property, Ma'am?' The woman stared stiffly. 'Or the price of it,' the man continued thickly as they remained silent for a while, not understanding.

'Prop-property? Pr-price?' Terna gasped.

'It's a fair demand, I say. Come on with it!' the coarse creature snapped.

'Explain yourself, make yourself clearer!' Madge ordered him. The man reddened. Then the more civilised looking of them stepped closer and addressed them. ''Tis his wife that's missin' a trifle, that's what it is now then, Mrs, or Miss. I – I don't believe that any suspicion should be thrown on – anyone here.'

'You hold your tongue, you dunderhead,' the man called Scundy shouted, 'sayin' what I was told I am. You were never told. I know you. You gave me two pints to pretend and lie, so you did, so innocent people would pay for the loss. There you have it now.'

The first speaker hated being exposed and looked daggers as the two withdrew to the street. Terna began to breathe again and was overjoyed that Madge was able to reassure her that there was nothing amiss during her absence. It was an inflexible rule that the Canning children mixed with youngsters of character, irrespective of class or creed. Escapades *can* occur during the natural freemasonry that exists between young children. The bright memories of recent travels vanished at the thought, for it was as if an iron weight had been flung at her only a few minutes before as Scundy had been starting his ruse

... his dupe! How she missed Peter! And poor Madge's presence was like an angel's veil before one of a family who used and exploited people to their own advantage, generally.

At this point the proceedings became dramatic. The now confused husband of the loser of the trifle was required by a messenger who stated that his woman was being removed to become the mother of premature twins after their own daughter had owned up to the theft, valued at a few pence. The other man followed them muttering something about 'makin' a wicked fool of himself an' *everywan* else.' Scundy had to travel further to find the grabber of the trifle, as supposed, or possibly make another bid for easy money. Terna remarked that: 'thieves' can be so deceiving from what I have just seen. One would need to be a chief detective to cope with such cases.' The women stayed together that time, Madge saying that the man with the loud voice was the better versed in their kind of job.

By next morning the frightened women were quite tranquil, each following up her own plan for the day. Peter had already rung with news of their safe arrival and that the children romped all day happily, even though they missed their mother terribly.

Even though fully invigorated after her cycling tour and the interesting variety in Kay's place, the Glenmark atmosphere threatened to get her out of tune. For days she just sat around after her morning's chores. Madge felt uneasy. The weather had broken by this time and all outdoor pleasures had to be abandoned. Even Madge's short runs from the house proved to be impossible for every time that she ventured it began to rain cats and dogs. And once she was caught in great sheets of lightning and a thunderstorm. For a week the pent-up skies appeared to burst in a deluge and the over-charged air was stiflingly oppressive ... it was the second time that fear gripped them. Then a welcome change. The rain fell in torrents and the skies cleared by degrees. So numerous were the raindrops glimmering in the sudden sun that the back garden looked like a crystalline mass from the windows, and the ash tree resembled a silver umbrella. The shade below netted the quivering gleams of light from above. Oozy noises came from the saturated flowers and vegetables as if glad to be refreshed. The lettuces looked greener. The blossoms on the tall potato stalks threw out extra pink leaves. Cabbages showed that they had been strengthened by the flood, their strong veins well marked. Only delicate, recent transplants resented the downpour, resented it so much that they buried themselves in the dark, deep clay and in a broad field outside the mearing, uncut, over-ripe grass fell in a tawny carpet.

Terna spent an hour outside almost spellbound at the change, Madge enjoyed her in this attitude, as if dedicated, as if rapt in the theme that she loved and yet drinking in the plain scene. Some roses hung like velvet pads on the trees and new buds like lipsticks.

At last as she descended the steps from the garden she thought: that rose is an entity. I am a nonentity until I make a name for myself. Then she saw that the old man was looking and listening closely, and of course, rawly resenting her happy state. A row of low shrubs divided their gardens. Giraffy found a natural peace too trying on his usually belligerent cast of mind. He began by making little human grunts to make her aware of his presence. The grunts ended in a series of short coughs that held angry, repudiating hints. Then he began to pace the concrete walks. With a coarse shuffling of the feet he paused, now and then, to peer aggressively around his property (including Canning's) as if he were on a tour of inspection, as if some intruder had trespassed.

Muttering to himself then, he entered his summer-house and searched diligently for further tracks. He stretched his scallopy arms into every corner and felt the little seats carefully, only to find that spiders had been busy with gossamer strands and that rats and mice had found some seat covers tasty enough to tear since his last visit to it. At the sight of him, Terna went indoors as he was the colour of whipped egg whites with temper. The two discreet women viewed him from inside. Still making squeaky screeches he doubled his steps and studied the tops of his huge boots while his expression conveyed that he wanted to hit somebody. And unluckily, at that moment, the Cannings' huge, black cat (an aristocrat to her ears) crossed his garden. Then the enraged giant rushed at her and kicked her into the air with maniacal delight. The injured animal mewed pitifully and fell on her back on the concrete. Finally she made her way to a sheltered place in his wild garden, where in the course of an hour two beautiful kittens – one of them alive – were found by him.

The onlookers fully realized that this was a psychological moment in the life of the frenzied man. Terna wondered how Peter would have reacted to the incident. She knew, of course, that had she ventured into his grounds and handed him a sweep-ticket, the infuriated creature might have changed, for next to his own life money was like the breath of life. He talked of nothing else while he was awake.

When Terna and Madge had taken lunch they decided to get into the country and return at nightfall. Madge took her knitting. Though the pastures had been soaked through they dried quickly again. Madge spread a thick rug over a great, flat rock in a field and there they sat. The sparsely-treed, mountain hills lay quite near.

'I am so relieved as well as amused that the piece of trickery about the pinched article finished as quickly as it began,' Terna said.

'Well, of course you are, and delighted that the man stood up for you as he sobered up, pricks of conscience, I suppose. All is well that ends well.' She picked up her knitting.

When Madge was not speaking the older woman's thoughts turned to Peter, Gay, Vane, Blitz and Jay in Carfort. The much improved circumstances there were a great source of satisfaction to the whole circle of relatives and in-laws, also outside well-wishers whose parents remembered the first change for the worse in it. Madge had been there once, and liked what she saw in the way of advancement. 'Oh! she cried, 'I'll never forget the healthy breezes in that grand, high country. One could almost see into the Midlands on a clear, sunny day.' So much for that part of South Galway!

Relaxation must come to an end like action and when the first chill of evening blew in their faces, Madge acted on her own initiative and rose to go home. She folded her knitting as Terna lifted the rug, and whatever backward glance she gave she noticed that the rock was infested with ants, some dead and some alive. Imagine their sitting on those without being stung – even with the rug! Terna saw that the rug was free of them before they departed.

And then what an evening to follow! While Madge prepared tea Terna filled the house with flowers and melodies, especially the tunes her kind helper liked best: *I hear you calling me, When you come to the end of a journey, When I come home on leave, Over the rainbow*, and others. Not forgetting a composition that Terna had written on Martin de Porres, the Saint-to-be. Madge insisted that she play many Irish dance tunes, the same as visiting bands played in the local dance hall. When that session ended, Madge obliged with a bout of step-dancing which went on until a soft knock outside put an end to it.

When Terna opened the door a young, dark-haired girl stood there. She was not a stranger to Madge and was brought up in a religious home. Before she opened her mouth, the woman knew that she had a problem of some kind, for her serious eyes fell on the ground and then strayed to the back window through which a host of tall flowers smiled from without. Terna was beginning to wonder at it all and exchanged glances with Madge when the girl spoke.

'I know I shouldn't bother you, Ma'am! or even expect you to listen, but my mother bought a hat a while ago, and now she sees one of our neighbours wearing one exactly the same.'

'And so?' Terna asked, quietly.

'Well, mother is really mad that anybody else has the same hat, but she can't return hers as she has worn it a few times already.' The three women stood looking at each other, Terna hoping that she should not figure in such a situation ever again. Regardless of her feelings, the girl asked:

'What do you advise her to do, Ma'am?'

Terna composed herself as best she could. She would have liked something to hold on to for that passing moment. The girl waited, expectant. Then, after a few deep breaths, Terna asked the colour of the hat. The girl said it was brown. Then the adviser's face changed: the girl's mother should purchase another hat of the same make and material, but of a different colour. She told the now-relieved girl to keep a look-out for the wearer of the hat so that she herself could remind her mother to wear the duplicate, though different one, on the same occasions, as they lived so near each other. She finished by saying that all the viewers could say was, though the hats were alike, they looked different.

Terna's proposal and comment were well received, the light of satisfaction shone in the girl's eyes as she left with much gratitude, though her adviser thought it all stupid, and supposed that the mother of the girl must have had simulated virtues only.

'A female Solomon you are,' Madge smiled.

'It would not be nice not to suggest something to the girl,' Terna pointed out. They were ready for more tea then, and after it Terna attended to her correspondence. Her Carfort, Cratton and Kilcross friends came first usually. In her letter Fay mentioned that the dark-eyed young man of Terna's single days had confided to her that he would lead an indulgent and careless life when he did not get the girl he wanted! Terna burned the letter quickly, commenting that wrongdoing would be in it until the stars failed. One of the following days Terna accompanied a friend to visit an old church in the outskirts of the parish of Glenmark and was constantly amused at the original yarns the buxom woman told her. She also stated that she had been having trouble with her husband's perpetual drinking bouts, day and night – years of it. Terna suggested that she might tell the offender that he should keep the last moments of his life always before his mind. Strange to relate, the addict's chronic condition changed for the better, though he was really a sullen bully during the transition period; and he was soon the man he used to be, even developing a disgust for the very stench of drink. Terna was glad over it, she was doing somebody good ... despite a possible erratic relapse by the reformed one.

Good news of the holidaymakers arrived almost daily. The two people at home felt happy in other people's well-being. The days were flying and Terna looked forward. Then Jock and Fay informed them they had had another addition to their family – a girl – and that they intended to call her Terna. So the delighted aunt dispatched congratulations and a gift to her namesake. And at the same time a cousin announced her intention to marry a certain fellow who idolised her. Both lived in Cratton and were around the same age. Terna used to visit there in her younger days and was always charmed at the close trees around the place and the ferns smothering yards of ground where sheep had to nip harder for a mouthful of grass.

Then, out of the blue, a lovely, college girl whom Gay had met and liked, turned up on the doorstep. The girl's visit was a great surprise, but Terna welcomed her warmly and treated her the way a late teenager liked. On the second day of her visit, the pretty visitor opened her heart to her hostess and even confided in her; she had fallen for a no-good, but she thought that he would change through her own good example and fidelity to him.

The tears showed in Terna's eyes. 'Then choose a worthy man, dear!' The little guest never expected this and she was crestfallen for the moment. 'Never marry a man in the hope of reforming him. It would be as well for you to try to tame the river in Glenmark. Go for future safety! The world will be always full of desirable men.'

'Oh! Missis Canning, nobody speaks like you,' the young girl declared without the explosiveness and defiance that are expected from her age group. And by the next evening, over a tasty meal, she admitted that the particular character mentioned would always place his own interests first and would pass through life as a chancer. Young as she was, the face-to-face discourse with Gay's mother made her suddenly mature. Terna's way of saying things was convincing and all the more to the young, looking for an opinion. Terna spoke with her as if it was Gay who wanted candour and truth, and when the day of departure dawned for the student she almost begged to be invited again. When she arrived home and started college, she would, she assured Terna, wipe out even the memory of a worthless man.

When that day passed Terna summed up the heartbreak story of some:

> *Hearts do not break as yet,*
> *Only in life's last breath.*

Though she herself loved the word 'life' she was always aware of the uncertainty and urgency of death. Life, the allotted span of sharps and trebles over spalls and pebbles, increasing in speed for a certain cycle, and then beginning to move with serenity and dignity to its end and a soul's rebirth.

Peter and the children mentioned that they would return on a certain date and Terna went to meet them by bus to the railway station. Even though Madge and herself had made full preparation there were some last-minute tasks to attend to, such as airing beds and blankets. Full of happy excitement she sat beside a very large lady with a calculating expression. Then she began to feel ill, and as she grew paler the woman requested her to leave, in a tall, bank-balance accent. So curtly condescending was her tone that the sick passenger wondered if she had bought the bus.

It so happened that Terna had not to leave and reached the journey's end safely. But the opposite happened. Peter and the darlings had not arrived and that meant another hour's wait. So she made her way to a hotel and ordered a light meal as she did not fancy a heavy one in her stuffy condition. After that she rang Madge and explained all. When she swallowed a tablet she felt heaps better, and stood to watch leaves fluttering on a small tree.

The evening was glorious. The faint rustle of early Autumn played in the treetop, and here and there little half-brown, half-green crispy leaves rolled along like playful kittens. Then she started to walk to kill time.

Waiting, at any time, is not pleasant. She passed by a bank, a post office, a day school for boys and a hospital run by nuns. A magnificent climber was rampant on a private house painted white with the bottom and the window sills a clear blue. She reckoned as she walked and retraced her steps to the station, finishing as the train steamed in. It was not crowded and Peter and the children were on the spot waving five hands at her and ready to jump through the windows. Greetings and embraces followed and when their bags and luggage were secure the family started for home.

The children were tanned an even brown. Gay grew tall and looked as if she had spent a month cruising. Blitz's hair had turned a lighter gold while Vane's cheeks were like ripe peaches. Of the four children, little Jay looked the least invigorated. When they arrived in Cane Street Madge's ready smile showed her genuine joy at seeing them all again. They were regaling each other avidly when some fumbling at the front door brought Madge to open it. There on the threshold stood the two men who had come to dupe before. They were sober and apologetic, and while Madge stared angrily, Terna was giving a brief account of them to Peter. 'They have tried to dupe,' she said loudly. 'One of them was not so bad,' she added.

The policeman in Peter saw all at once and he made a bee-line for the door shouting: 'Let me at them!' He swung himself at the men and demanded an explanation.

'We're here to apologise to Mrs Canning. Leave it at that, will ye, like a good gintleman? You've a fine time, Sir! You might give *us* a chance, Sir!'

At this point Terna appeared at the door and bowed them off politely, and on account of the time that was in it, Peter let the whole thing drop at his wife's request and the men departed, unsure still and confused.

Peter and Terna returned to the living room when the Cratton, Carfort and Kilcross presents were being unpacked. Terna trembled with joy as she laid her hands on a large, very old volume of the poetical works of famous authors. Officer Canning, as a Glenmark farmer called him, also carried a load of vegetables from Carfort, the best the place was seen to produce in many years. And he had something else up his sleeve. As there were four days leave of which he had not availed himself some weeks before his annual leave, he decided to use it. The authorities were understanding, and in accordance with his plans he informed the family, Madge included, that they were to spend the next three days by the sea in Salthill, a leading holiday spot in County Galway. Terna was flushed with pleasure during the minimum preparation for all and at the prospect of turning her back on Glenmark once more. Everything was much of a muchness there. So the house in Cane Street had been vacated and locked in less than two hours the next day. Looking at the happy family set out, made one forget that there was a war on. The Cannings seemed to have a knack of enjoying themselves. They grew browner hourly at the sea, and Jay's tender skin blistered with the salty air. Blitz waded like a duck in the warm water. Peter said she was like a sea nymph in bathing suit and long, wet hair. Gay and Vane stretched on the sands and read their favourite comics while Jay kept very near his mother all the time.

Terna was like a fuse during their stay. She collected impressions, hints and ideas for future composition and those literary fragments were very suitable when perused. Peter watched and understood when she walked by the sea at twilight, when the sun had gone and the children rested in the hotel under Madge's supervision. As usual, the more subdued music of the waters and a faint touch of the sombre appealed to her. She always held that she had richer thoughts by a deserted seaside than anywhere else on earth. Just then two long-legged, stationary cranes pecked at each other and parted. The lights from passing cars made luminous patches on the dark water and less than half a league away to the left, the frame of an ill-fated boat was barely from the shore where she stood. The wreck was hemmed in by rocks.

The next day the Cannings were to take pictures of it after viewing it with binoculars. With this in mind Terna and Peter joined their family and planned the next part of their programme. They found Madge and her four charges pleasantly tired, the younger ones fatigued enough for bed. So when the noisy procedure was over the parents and Madge slipped away to the cinema.

## CHAPTER 16

# *More Togetherness*

Next day the Cannings set off after breakfast to view the wreck of what once looked like a graceful bird with shining plumage on the waters of the Corrib and the bay.

'It is no mirage,' Peter remarked, 'but the sorry remains of a good vessel.'

Vane was so moved that he said: 'Oh! Mammie! how I would love to be a Captain and travel the broad seas. I pity that boat down there when I think of the thousands of miles of water that it once covered.'

'Well, Vane, things and people can only go so far in this world.' Gay reminded him wisely. 'We will all look like that some day.'

They stayed around until it was time to return to the hotel for lunch and after a very satisfactory one Madge prepared the children for a matinee while their parents sat on one of the seats provided, enjoying the loud lashing on the surfy rocks. People of all ages who preferred a late holiday passed by them on the promenade, some young people linked and chatting, while others lay like sardines between the hills of sand further away.

Terna had to bear in mind that re-opening day was near and the younger members of the family would go to school with unsmiling faces. Gay, of course had been fixed in by telephone in a well-known convent of the Loreto order in the Midlands of Ireland, even a month before. Gay appeared very much grown-up and responsible at the prospect of getting away on her own. She had a particularly good manner, to quote the Headmistress of the school later on. This was gratifying to her parents.

Peter and Terna spent almost two hours with half-closed eyes, and

71

then they decided to have a swim to waken themselves up. They had scarcely started when happy shouts from the shore attracted their attention. Madge and the charges were back, and Terna directed them to wait on the shore until she arrived with Peter. Madge never swam so she missed nothing. While she herself was swimming, Terna composed the beginning of the poem: *With the waves in Salthill*. Then suddenly Vane was missing from the circle. Madge was almost beside herself. Had Vane ventured into a deep spot? The word ran round and helpful people searched and called his name. Gay and Blitz ran the whole length of the promenade as far as the pier, calling, calling. But Terna knew a surge of faith and in spirit she knelt in the little, pink room in Carfort. And not in vain, for it clearly occurred to her then that Vane would be found. Blindly, she pulled on her clothes and headed for the hotel, giving the information as calmly as she could, while Peter was angrily correcting Madge for losing touch with the boy. The hotel people had not seen a sight of him since after lunch, so Terna turned away ready to weep. She went towards the entrance to contact her family when a boy's pleasant voice fell on her ears. 'Never mind, Mammie! I am here beside you, they told me you were looking for me. I got a lift to the old boat, I wanted to see it again, and I ran back. See, I am out of breath.'

The happy woman could not speak and when they joined the rest later they found them fairly shaken. Only Madge spoke. 'I knew Vane had the sense to mind himself.'

Terna's next gesture was to treat them all to ice cream with sherry on top, for the holiday feeling was threatening to wear off with the shock. And it was not until they had partaken of a meal later that they could speak to each other naturally. Vane himself cheered them at every word. So evening saw them all together, glad to be alive and grateful for many things. Next Peter proposed a visit to the Links for a game of golf. Terna spent an hour reading to the children while Madge went off on her own to visit a nurse in a hospital. Blitz would listen forever, but Vane and Jay grew tired after a few pages. 'Tell us what happened, Mammie, before you come to the end,' Vane would request her, 'I want to have a kick of a ball on the beach.'

'And what of Blitz?'

'Ah, she is only a girl,' he reasoned.

Terna reluctantly agreed but ordered Vane to stay within eyesight all the time. To this he agreed and was soon speeding along the beach to join the players, his long legs like white hurleys as he ran. Quiet descended on the others and they were content to sit and look at the little groups of foreigners who stayed so much to themselves, their toughly-built bodies the colour of very fresh beef, from over a fortnight's exposure to the rays of a Galway sun. The dark-skinned tourists had nothing to fear.

When the boys felt exhausted Vane came to his mother's side at once and rested until the familiar voice of Peter hailed them. He was standing by a car which a friend lent him to take them all for a spin to an outlying place in the wild and forever beautiful stretches of Connemara further west. 'You are forever springing pleasant surprises at us, Peter!' Terna began. 'Nothing to what I get,' he said in a good-natured way, 'but do not forget that this is our last day here, do not lose track of time.'

'Aw, Daddy!' Blitz cried, 'can't we go home tomorrow?'

'Into the car, dears, and we will collect Madge at the hospital first,' was his answer. As they climbed in, the slanting sun bothered their eyes through the windscreen, and Jay hid his head in Terna's arm until the car started. Sometimes the glare would be obscured by a high hedge only to flash again. Then they were at Madge's venue and took a different road to the one decided on. Every turn of the wheels was an added thrill, especially to the young ones, and Terna made up her mind to lie back and forget about words, rhythms and metres for the time being. Peter used to sing snatches of *The Queen of Connemara* on the way. Speed was possible in that isolated tract as there was little traffic. By the time they drew up it was time to turn back to the hotel and prepare for the journey to Cane Street and Glenmark. It was a rush and Peter exclaimed on the way: 'This time tomorrow I shall be in uniform and possibly Barrack Orderly.'

'Do not mention it, yet, Peter!' Terna begged, and they were silent for a mile or so, knowing the intense hatred Terna had for the official. Then they found themselves at home and right there, as if posted to it, stood an elderly member of the travelling class, a woman with eyes as pale as her face. The woman begged an alms wistfully, at the same time bestowing benisons on Terna without looking at the rest. Terna opened her coat and let it slide off her shoulders, kindly though dramatically, into the appealing woman's hands. The woman left, not believing her eyes and muttering her thanks.

# CHAPTER 17

# First Parting

Terna grew very busy, for Gay's school outfit had to be in readiness with all her clothing marked with her name. She also required a new school trunk. She was constantly in attendance on her mother, reminding her of the more trivial things for her first term away. The new studies would not be difficult for her, as she had already received private tuition. Later, Terna took different pictures of the whole family to be enlarged later.

Other than for business or vacation, Gay's leaving was the first break in the circle. Terna gave the order to a local shop and paid cash down to the draper. A daughter of the same people travelled all the eighty miles in the train with Gay. This was accidental.

While Madge was fixing in blankets and sheets little Jay was heard crying his heart out in an adjoining room. 'Why is the sweet lady going?' All consoled him, but he still cried and cried. 'Shall the sweet lady be long away?' Terna consoled him as best she could, but he refused to stop crying, and when at last his parents left him to Madge, he had a final burst of tears. When, at last, his parents left with Gay, Madge carried him to buy his favourite sports book and sweets.

Gay's going made an awful difference for she was like a second mother in the family. She had the right word at the right time for everybody, and was altogether a very clever and unassuming beauty. Vane and Blitz missed her just as much as Jay did, but they were old enough to understand that secondary education should be a 'must' for all of them.

'So, this is a glad day as well as a sad day for all of us, then?' Vane commented.

'Well, yes, Vane! But most days are like that, aren't they?'

'Nearly. It is true. That is why Mammie has not the smile on her face all the time.'

'That is it.'

At this point Jay began to settle down, and, after a while was even full up of going to school with his brother and sister. To cheer them up that day, Madge played records, told them stories and showed them how good children acted in their homes and outside. The children benefited, for Blitz washed up, Vane fetched turf and Jay did small messages for her.

All their old equilibrium was restored. A single girl acting as substitute for an orderly mother was a test, though it was nothing new for her since she joined the family that she liked so well. It *is* true that she hardly ever had an idle moment, but the Cannings were liberal, not in one way, but in every way, even in the matter of her days off. Madge had come from a large family, so she understood children and liked them. On that particular night when the children went to bed, she sat on a settee with the doors leading to the bedrooms wide open in case they needed her. The radio was on low, and she passed a few pleasant hours between that and reading the daily papers. Outside, the early night was so calm that there could have been a great, plush canopy tightly over Glenmark. And, higher up, the stIll stars looked down as if they were keeping a happy watch.

The woman parted the curtains to look out. She valued those moments though she did not fancy solitude at all, though she was bound to be influenced, somewhat, by her mistress. Then she slipped out the back for some fuel, as, calm though the night was, there was a chilly wind blowing just then. She lolled around until the extra heat of the kindling fire caused her to nod off, but her doze was soon interrupted by the lights of a car on the front curtains.

Terna and Peter had landed. They opened the doors themselves as both carried keys. They were almost in the middle of the living room when Madge rose to fix things for them. One glance at Terna's face was enough for her.

The parting with Gay was harder on her than on Peter. Peter appreciated education from every angle. They both spoke of the nuns in glowing terms especially the Reverend Mother of the community, and were delighted that they had chosen the place for Gay. Gay herself had been very sensible from the first moment until they said goodbye.

Their home atmosphere relieved the parents, and Madge's wise, consoling words were good to listen to, and carried weight with her employers. After some time all three said goodnight and retired.

The morning after, everybody was considerate to each other. Vane stepped into Gay's shoes. Before and after school he would appear, as if from nowhere, to stand by his mother's side to help her, and to remind her of things. She did not need to be reminded to type the few lines that Gay had written the week before she left:

*My Mother*

*When I sit by a stream*
  *And see its ripples*
*Then my thoughts teem*
  *Of a lovable mother.*
*Mother's one of the first*
  *To visit God at morn*
*Tracing her steps again*
  *When the evening creeps.*
*Praying for all.*
*Oh may she live in peace*
  *To see the result of prayer!*
*May we be as she is,*
  *Kind always!*

*Gay*

Though Gay's lines had halting metre and imperfect rhythm and rhyming, they sprang from the depths of her thirteen-year-old soul. And it is possible that she was inspired by her mother's attendance at daily Mass, a habit she had since Vane was born.

Gay's people counted the hours until her first letter home was dropped into the box, and that important missive was read and re-read by each member of the family. Even Jay demanded that all the words should be explained in full to him, one by one. Anything the sweet lady said was always of the utmost importance to him.

'Well, when is she coming home?' he asked. He was informed that she had not mentioned that, when he said: 'Ah! I'll have to try to love school here until she comes back again.'

'Oh! you'll have her when Santa Claus comes around again,' he was told. He grew happier. The house was very quiet during school hours. Jay, being the youngest, came home first every day.

Once he rushed to his mother to hand her a drawing that he had done on his first day at school and which his teacher had kept for him. It was the drawing of a cat sitting:

Terna decided to keep Jay's attempt forever, and enquired of his father if he thought that Jay should become an architect like his cousin, Shay, in Dublin. And even as she talked, the first lines of a composition – verses about the Saint of France, Thérèse of Lisieux – began to take shape in her mind. The short work appeared later in the official organ of the Carmelites of San Antonio, Texas. The publication was a National Bi-monthly by the Discalced Carmelite Fathers. The date was the September-October Issue, 1948.

It was then that Peter decided on another break, so they went to see an old relative of his in the east of Ireland. The lady had kept remarkably well, considering that she was almost an octogenarian. She had a strong resemblance to Peter.

There was pleasant news when they came home. Gay had got the highest marks in poetry in school. And to add to it, their daughter mentioned that she would be home for Hallowe'en and her mother's birthday and that she looked forward to it.

Then, right after that, Terna and Madge plunged into preparations for the visit of Peter's brother from the States. By November there was a proper plethora of presents between Michael's and those that were sent on with him. Gifts were of especial importance to the Cannings, for they aimed at the practical as well as catering for taste. Gay had much to tell of her new life in the Loreto School. Her music teacher, Mother Cecelia, had made a lasting impression on her young pupil, and the latter valued highly a small packet of clay from the grave of Saint Cecelia in Rome which the nun had given her at her first music lesson. Gay's gift to her mother was a pair of fur slippers. Peter presented her with a Parker pen, and Blitz a writing compendium. Vane's gift was a book of short prayers, and little Jay, out of the whole world, a piggy bank.

Michael drew up on the last day of Gay's stay, but they had time for a short outing. Her eyes were moist as she left, amid reminders of her next home-coming. That helped to raise her spirits. Her uncle was very pleased at her application to her studies. No sooner had she gone when Blitz fell ill with over-eating, nothing more. Fasting for a day and rest in bed was the cure. During his stay Michael admitted to Terna that he was of the same opinion as Lord Dunsany concerning her literary features, that they were *sensible*. And while he read a few verses aloud, Terna was, undoubtedly, reading a passage mentally from the appreciative words that she would write when her brother-in-law would no longer be alive. For he had an inward complaint that would eventually finish him, though he was physically able then.

They paid a visit to her husband's people's tomb in the south of Cavan, saw the towering headstones over another member of their family and the suitably inscribed names of his three medical relatives, all of whom had served as surgeons in the Royal Navy. She found herself adding word for word in relation to Michael:

> *Forget-me-nots are growing on a scene*
> *Where the hills of Cavan mourn in their green ...*

as a beginning only. Before Michael had emigrated he had left Cavan to settle in Westmeath with his family. So he sailed away on the *Mauretania* at the end of the only Winter holiday he had ever taken in Ireland.

By this time, Blitz and Jay had become great pals. She hardly ever let him out of her sight, and she kept him like a tin soldier, as clean and bright as the buttons on their father's uniform. Sometimes Jay would rebel at being constantly supervised from the angle of his skull cap to the last letter of his headlines. But Blitz had her way until his mother changed it. Blitz and Jay were often seen shopping together, looking very responsible. Once Terna asked him which shops they bought in. He told her, and then remarked that they did not bill anything because *she* did not. And I said: 'Put paper on the things, please,' he added seriously.

Gay had scarcely settled in again when she had a surprise visit from her father and Jay, both wearing their new pullovers that Terna had knitted for them. Peter had had this treat up his sleeve for a while for his pleasing second son. From an early age the boy had a turn of fun that always entertained, and he was quite an advanced thinker. Then Blitz began to make friends of her own, and often enjoyed the company of a young clergyman who explained all the things that puzzled her young mind. Sometimes her questions were tiring, on his own admission. Some Fridays, he treated her to the local cinema, little books and ribbons for her hair.

Terna preferred the rich cakes she made herself to the lighter confectionery. Peter had a sweet tooth. The cakes she set about mixing while her husband and son were away were the same as the ones she usually posted to Gay every fortnight or so, not quite as rich as her confections for nuns' feast-days.

She also made time to visit friends in the country for a few hours to have a look about in unfamiliar scenes. The next evening she was pleasantly aroused by the arrival of Peter and Jay. Peter was his relaxed self, but Jay's fine eyes showed that he had shed tears. He spoke of the nuns' admiration for their knitted garments. Terna always chose an intricate pattern, and after a few rows she would be able to knit and converse without making a mistake in the pattern. She would tell Vane that she was offering every stitch so that a sin would be prevented somewhere at that moment. God listens to our wishes, she told him. 'Well, can't I ask Him to cure me if I ever fall ill? And won't He?'

'If He wishes to, Vane! That is all.'

# CHAPTER 18

# *Intentions*

Vane was hoping for everything of the best for his immediate family, and he maintained that every action had a religious foundation, and when engaged in work with his father he would request him to do it all in honour of the saint of the day. He made a very thorough preparation for his confirmation, and, though he faltered before answering one of the questions, he had all the necessary knowledge beforehand. On every Good Friday from that date he stayed three hours in the church in honour of The Passion.

Terna grew amused when he told her he would be a boxer, raising his arm to his father and asking him if he had a good muscle. Vane liked a challenge but thought that there were too many 'whys' and 'ifs' in life. He was greatly cheered when Peter told him that he had taken out an insurance for him and that it would mature when he was twenty-one years old. As they talked Jay rushed in telling them of the chairoplanes being in Glenmark, for the pony races to be held there. So, between school, lessons and pleasures the new generation of Cannings could hardly keep track of time.

Gay informed them that she intended to have two of her front teeth extracted before her next holiday. And soon Peter decided to visit his brother who was his senior by eight years, and who lived in Dublin. He was the exact opposite of Peter in manner and outlook, and hardly ever made time for visiting anybody. His sons were then going through college and university. The sons later married and emigrated to America, England and one to Northern Ireland. Three of their wives were Irish and one German.

In Peter's job, he had limited time for long-distance travel, so he always managed to leave Cane Street very early in the morning and return before midnight on free days. The visit to his brother was the same, where he found him ailing. Vane went too, and his uncle soon declared that he would lay the nations on that nephew's shoulders, something that had been said before by a doctor who had met him for the first time, two years earlier. A week after their return from Dublin, Vane went by bus to Galway City to purchase a toast-rack for Terna. She felt obliged for she was putting the finishing touches to a short play called *Secret for Three*, which was to be staged by a Donegal producer, Antony Timmoney who had much experience of such work. Terna had contacted him through the *Derry Journal*. He was in his sixties then.

More news of Gay: she had her name down to sit for Cafferty's examination. And Vane had won a prize for Question Time in the local school. Then, intending to join a real boxing club in Glenmark, he got into his first long trousers. Oh! he felt so manly! Only he flinched and grew self-conscious when Blitz threw her expressive eyes on him as if he were some kind of curiosity. But he forgot that in a matter of minutes and fled to his club.

Extra money is always welcome. When Peter had changed a cheque for a considerable amount and Vane, Blitz and Jay lined up with various demands, Peter settled it by buying new shoes for them instead. And expensive bootees were sent to Gay, also. The others spent the evening fitting theirs.

But right on top of their rejoicing the news of the illness of their Uncle Jay's young wife clouded everything. She had just been told of her malady by the doctors. She had cancer and it was the incurable kind. She had already left for a Dublin hospital. Terna went to Cratton then, and all the way she wished that Gay was with her for the sake of encouraging ideas and mother-and-daughter exchange, for they had a good relationship. By the time she arrived in Cratton, Jay, Babe's husband, looked as if he had not grasped the diagnosis fully. She left it to him to talk of it, and she learned that he fully expected that an operation was all she wanted to be cured. She never discussed the worst with him at all, but stayed on to help.

Young Jay in Glenmark had a habit of butting in and saying things as he felt like it. Terna was told later that he went into every shop in town in her absence and repeated the Christmas Story as if he were paid to do it – in his own words: how God came down from high up and was born in a poor, cold cave, a *miserable* bed, how a cow warmed him while strangers adored him and wondered, and that he shivered. Listeners told him that his story would be received better nearer Christmas but there was no preventing him. It was a daily occurrence almost. And when his mother finally returned she did not know whether to laugh or grow angry when she heard of it.

Blitz helped to erect the Christmas Crib in Glenmark, that year, though she caught a bad cold in the old church. She grew feverish and was confined to bed for a week. Gay was a wonder for the whole term at home, the way she showed off her skill at cooking and baking, adding her new knowledge to what Terna had taught her. Her parents provided the ingredients after so she could take a large cake back with her.

Peter saw that Terna would appreciate a different gift that he had in mind for her. With the longer days approaching rural excursions would be first on the list, so he gave her a Raleigh bicycle. Terna thought it ideal. She would be able to squeeze in a spin between lunch and tea, and cover more ground in less time than she could with her old machine.

When the festivities were over, Blitz well again and Gay departed, Peter was listed for taking the tillage in a certain area of Glenmark. He dreaded the cold but the extra work meant extra money. The following months were exactly the same as far as the family activities went, and home life became more routine. Then a strange face appeared on the scene, in the person of Peter's eldest sister who walked in through the front doorway with a casual 'hello' just as if she had come every day for years! Alice had married rather late in life in America and had never known the music of a child's laughter in her wealthy home. Glenmark was cast in the warm stillness of late July when the hushed nights reminded Terna of sleeping doves. Alice loved the heat but Terna grew languid at midday, and lost her inertia only when the cool of evening spread its first fragrance around. The darkness crept in so slowly in those golden days, that perfect cycle, that the dark-lover experienced a certain regret that her venue in the garden was no longer available for secretive urges. The last time lunar light had spoiled the moment for her. Then memories crowded into her mind, running bog waters, windy woods, restful fields and the faint, bubbling music of distant streams in the south County Galway of her childhood. And she felt compensated, at least.

In this frame of mind she was confronted by Alice who spoke first. 'Do you ever intend to abandon your cultural tastes?' Terna was taken aback and remained silent for a short time.

'That is a loaded question, Alice! I would need to live to be a hundred to answer it. I am what I am, at the present and I may be what I am.'

'You would be much better off with another outlook,' the practical soul reminded her. 'Women should be light, amusing people, not sober musers.'

'Oh! what a flimsy view of them, and you yourself the soul of sobriety!' Her visitor smiled and began to write a letter to her husband.

When there was a week of her holiday left her niece, Gay appeared to spend some time with her Aunt Fay and Uncle Jock. Her leaving coincided with her old aunt's departure from Cane Street. Before Gay left, Blitz promised her that she would join her later and bring Jay with her if all went well. Blitz always talked and acted as if she loved leading. She was vexed when she had not been able to strew flowers and lead the procession the year before.

Two things stood out for Terna that year – The Holy Year. The gesture of His Holiness, Pope Pius XII, in sending her a medal of commemoration and his blessing. Following this, she had a slender volume of verse published: *Halcyon Days*. The publisher was English. On receiving copies she gave complimentary ones to some people. Though her family read them they did not memorize any of them, and none of the verses was of a tiresome length. Vane was really a candid critic, suggesting in an amateur way that she should switch from the Nature themes to everyday ones.

The next interesting events were that Vane sat for a scholarship in a well-known college in the country, did well, but was deprived of a place as the people running the college gave preference to their own boys. And Gay had done her musical theory examination with good results.

Clouds again. Mara's baby girl had died suddenly from respiratory trouble at a month old. Peter grieved for her as she was the living image of his late mother. He sent a letter of sympathy to his sister who had already four sturdy children.

Blitz, Jay and Gay returned home together on the very day that a huge parcel of games, goodies and wearables of all sorts had been posted on to them in Gay's name. Their delight and curiosity can be imagined as they tore open the box. Ah! two of the silk frocks and a velvet one were pink, rose and cerise. 'No more unbecoming colours to your red-gold and blonde hair,' Terna regretted. Though she settled that quickly. The girls could wear contrasting colours with the frocks, belts, hair bands or boleros. That would soften the clash. There was also an invitation to Gay which she could not accept, for the party was over by the time she came home. There was a packet of stamps for her, too, for she had become an avid collector by then.

It surprised Terna to see the children swinging back to the way things were before Gay went away to school, and Blitz preparing two recitations with the air of an expert for a concert to be held in the Community Centre. One of the pieces was about a cat. Before the concert date, however, Gay decided against going and Blitz thought it too late to stay up. One of the recitations was written specially for her by Terna: *What somebody thinks about Blitz*. Terna had a work about the stigmatist, Rose Ferron of America, on hands then. She titled it: *Love Lies Bleeding*.

Back to a business break now. The six Cannings next sent the same number of Post Office Savings Account books to the General Post Office in Dublin to have the annual interest added in due course. The fact that their parents' amounts exceeded the younger members' did not pass unnoticed without comment by their second daughter, so her parents waxed indulgent and invested in a Cowboy outfit for her. And immediately it was obvious that the drive of envy was prompting Vane and Jay to complain, so Terna eased the situation by handing them a small note each for their next deposits.

The large sums of money were necessary, for the time and place were already fixed for Vane to start his secondary education. He had been receiving private tuition for some time from a Glenmark teacher. As Gay had done honours papers, he wished to do the same. He did not settle in as quickly as Gay did. The college was in the south of Ireland. And he was counting the hours from his first day there! He wrote more often than Gay. She went by the rules, but he used to write a few lines on his own to find out how his family was. His college was over two hundred miles away, and that meant that visits would be few and far between for his relatives.

Terna was already working on a cardigan with two colours for his birthday on 13 December. She also meant to include a cake with his name iced on it. And, as an afterthought she included another article, a hand-knitted scarf in his college colours. Their giant cat disappeared the day he went, after mewing wildly in his room for hours. After her son left Terna arranged with nuns of the Presentation Order for Blitz to attend as a day scholar in their National school, as Terna had heard of an excellent music teacher there. Already she herself had instilled an appreciation of both vocal and instrumental music in the children.

# CHAPTER 19

# *Angles*

Success after success was then taken for granted for a period of many years. The Cannings had no problems. Peter had kept in touch with the distant members of his family, and always nursed a secret ambition to see some of America one day. Some of the time his wife used to wonder how it would all finish. She would never allow herself to envisage anything else but the way they were. Time was for actuality with her. On and off she would commit short lyrics to paper, on simple subjects, and some of those were just as quickly deposited in the waste paper basket without giving them another thought. All through, there must have been between forty and fifty of those different compositions mislaid or lost. Most times, so many alternatives would rush into her mind that it would be a time of deciding which or whether, so, rather than grow addled, she would engage in manual work for a few hours and then sweep into the country on her Raleigh. The attractions of spaces never wore off. And, indeed, at a certain time she thrilled to the pleasant coolness on a broad bridge that spanned the river in Glenmark, near Sandy Height with the ancient trees opposite. Standing there, she compared it all with the rat race of the last city that she visited in England, London, and had a sordid recollection of the extremes of wealth and poverty there, of the sight of thousands of people tasting of the bitter and the sweet, some facing failure bravely and others giving up the battle to survive in the face of the greatest odds, even preferring to die quietly, to sink peacefully into a watery grave. On the road by the river, the happy cyclist observed a plaque which had been erected to the memory of a chemist who had been murdered there by the English police in the Anglo-Irish trouble. The 'Tans' as they were labelled in Ireland, played much the same role as mercenary soldiers; some of them had been servicemen. With her mind full of the unfair sufferings of the Irish people and their years of bondage, she concluded that such conditions can engender a slave-mentality.

Proceeding and considering the activities of the 'Tans' and their low morale, she never felt the miles, and had reached an out-of-the-way National School inside the Mayo border. The building was closed and was up for sale.

Then she had to frown for she saw what she disliked: a young man of about twenty years striving to free himself from the embraces of three females younger than himself. The youth was positively distressed and there was genuine relief in his face when he saw Terna approach. The girls stood and stared at her as if she intruded. The oldest woman's first reaction was loathing, but before she had time to pass, the youth said sharply: 'It's not their first time, Ma'am, and I'm not the only one.'

'Are you not, poor boy?' He moved slowly as if not sure of his steps, and then jumped over a small gateway into a rushy field and away. A brazen girl then pushed up to Terna. She had very thick lips that barely concealed her large, uneven teeth, which by no means showed a lack of calcium. 'Men are for women, and women are for men, you're old enough to know,' she grinned.

'Never mind her, Mrs! She's the only one of us who's ever talkin' of pubbin' and boys. We two are not as pushin' as *her* in any way. And that poor, fella! His wife hates him and this one keeps remindin' him of it, so he'll become fully estranged from his own one who's nearly ten years older than he is. That fella was trapped you know.'

Terna had had enough. 'A sign of the times', she told herself. She pushed her bicycle for half a mile or so, taking in the bare scenery in the fresh winds that were so stimulating in the odd gleam of a cool sun. Then she turned to look for a sight of the young man who had escaped, but the nearest hedges were high and cut off her view. She supposed that it had rained heavily on the place very recently, for there were soggy springs on the grass margin where she stood. She could see the roof of one of the three churches in Glenmark from there as she slowly headed for that little town of five streets. Her mind was still on the new laxity in behaviour that was gradually creeping in, as well as the breaking of vows so casually, and before she reached Cane Street she kept convincing herself that of all the maladies in the world to which flesh is heir none of them was as bad as a sick soul.

Rather soon after, Fay's husband's doctor diagnosed stomach ulcers and ordered a special diet for him for a certain period. The patient co-operated with the doctor all the way in the hope of obtaining a cure. Terna learned this from Vena's daughter who called with a pile of country produce from the most fertile fields in Carfort. Terna made her comfortable. And something that was highly valued and appreciated followed: a real photo of Saint Thérèse of France from an old priest pilgrim, and yet again there was an announcement that the salaries of members of the Garda Siochana were being increased. And pleasure of pleasures! Vane's first holiday from college with the further information that he had won the North Munster championship in a game in Limerick, to be followed by another prize for Christian Doctrine. The then Bishop of the diocese presented it. The results of Gay's music examination, Eighth Grade, gave her cause to smile.

So in the general well-being Peter made Terna invest in a new outfit for what he termed a family reunion, during which time a member of the teaching staff in Vane's college called to see him. Vane described him as one who took his work very seriously and expected the boys to do likewise. That night, and on subsequent nights, the four young Cannings contributed concert items to Peter's great delight. Passers-by often paused to listen to the youthful voices from one room and Gay's professional handling of Chopin's and others' works on the piano, from another.

A description of Vane. He had grown very tall and handsome, with that first sign of dawning manhood, change of voice. Terna understood when he would cease singing with a break in the notes. His shoulders were wide and of good proportion and he had a more studious look. Two things touched his mother deeply – his joy at the extra preparations for his homecoming and the mature way that he told Jay that he could have all his old mechanical toys and guns, as he himself had to concern himself with more serious things. Jay ran to tell Terna as if he had received a legacy in the toys.

When, at last, the fortnight passed, everything fell into the usual perspective. Gay and Vane were happy enough from the viewpoint that they were preparing for their future, that they were both interested in study, and in an honours course all through. For a week after, quiet notes like muffled echoes seemed to fill the house in Cane Street. 'The sweet lady gone to Lor-lor-eto.' Joy cried again and again. Then he sought comfort from Vane's wide assortment of toys.

While Vane had been home he visited country houses around Glenmark, and soon had the pleasure of presenting a sturdy, black kitten to his mother. It came from healthy stock and Terna was delighted that her dead pet had been replaced. She called the new one Pal. Between ringing and writing the next term flew for the Cannings. There was always something interesting, the best move being that when Gay was allowed home one weekend in the longer days, Terna, a friend and herself drove to see Vane during the College sports. Vane was much thinner, then. No doubt, the extra exercise in preparation for the games caused it. The three travelled through the night, for, having partaken of their repast in the College, they stayed on for hours and visited Shannon Airport on the way back, an extra seven miles or so.

Next morning, as Gay was leaving, the postman was delivering letters. One stated that Uncle Michael had again arrived in Ireland and was on his way to Glenmark. Actually, he had already visited a cousin who was a Parish Priest, and had stayed a few days with him at the Parochial house in the County Longford. At home, Terna was calling up pictures of what it would be like when Michael came, for it cannot be repeated often enough, that the unparalleled generosity of the older members of the Canning family almost amounted to a creed. And Alice had remembered, for Michael was soon doing the very thing that Terna had expected, removing the contents of the car outside and walking in already, with his old look of noble reliability and, oh! such a sickly, grey pallor! Her heart sank. He understood her feelings and proceeded to unpack, and she was right in what she felt about Alice for when she opened a tiny box, she found a silver flower inscribed: Saint Anthony's Lily. Then, it was Peter's turn, for he looked ten years younger already at seeing his brother again. So he and his wife opened their hearts and hands that time and managed a four-day run with their visitor, taking in a visit to their younger sister who had lost her little daughter. While the blood relations had a family chat, Terna began to cram her mind with literary constructions about people, things and places, and, of future grim necessity, the moving sentiments required for the remainder of the piece about the man who stood farther away with a kingly air, with whose best traits

Vane was so richly endowed. She walked slowly to join the others, telling herself that people were the most valuable assets in all creation! Watching their efforts, hopeful endurance, their approach to problems and their achievements, made her arrive at that conclusion.

In Cane Street once more, Terna could afford to be thrilled, but it was her turn to endure then, for Pal was lying dead outside their house as they pulled up. The cat had been crushed with a van only shortly before, for he was still warm. A word from Michael was enough to console her, for he referred to the unhappy incident as one of her little ups and downs. And even while they spoke, Peter hurried away with the half-mutilated body of her pet to bury it. 'Never refer to it,' Michael advised. Terna consoled herself with the idea that Vane would hunt up yet another feline friend for her. Michael had a full programme, for they travelled to Ashford Castle, Cong, to dine and relax. He loved the place and often drew up to admire and examine specimens of weeds and wildflowers peculiar to the district, regional flora he had never seen anywhere. He had seen sheets of wild poppies, scabious and tufts of comfrey on one occasion before. Poppies are self-sowers and multiply easily. Michael could describe things with such facility! and so ended the run to the West. After it, Terna felt exhausted, so the men took Blitz on a mystery tour. Fast driving made her mother rather dizzy. And Madge was glad of her help for they meant to relax after an early lunch, each in her own way, which they did.

# CHAPTER 20

# Moves and Thoughts

Relaxation to Terna meant resting physically for so long and no longer. She slipped away to her room and reappeared shortly with a notebook in which she wrote two questions: (1) Why do people hate Winter? She lay full stretch on a sofa, looking at the ceiling, saying in a mildly defensive monotone and writing, 'Winter, Winter, calm and loud in turns, of diamond clarity when a full moon's lips part in a brightening smile over dividing, amber seas in the congested valley of the earth spoilt with concrete buildings; mostly houses where human creatures live, many of whom never ask themselves why they were born, even in the winter of their lives …'

The drapes of night clung to her like a protector and allowed her to luxuriate to such a degree that she could forget the material world completely. (2) Why do worthy, admirable men, married and single, create opportunities to confess to a married woman that they desire her for themselves, and admit that they entertain a bold hope of marrying her one day regardless of her age? Oh! what a messy situation for a regulated mind to think about. Men ready to wreck the lives of so many others. Imagine a correct woman handling such pressing requests from time to time! Requests going beyond the bounds of reason altogether. Reproof, avoidance of certain occasions and instant flight on her part are the woman's safest measures, Terna found … Men get an impression, an impulse, and then an emotion. Men can be leeches when they are deep in the sweet idiocy of it all.

Madge had a meal ready then and the older woman laid the notebook aside and joined her. They had had a lovely day and had hardly looked once in each other's direction. 'Think of the many things we can enjoy, Madge!' and also a definite aspect of other-worldliness. 'And what is not today will be tomorrow.'

Madge smiled. 'That's what happiness is all about, Mrs!' she said. 'I notice that you can turn even sorrow to good account.'

'I use it, Madge! It matures us. Peter thinks so, too. Happiness can elude and we can never *persuade* ourselves that we are happy.'

Then an imperative knock had to be answered and Terna rose. She thought it was a ring from Peter, but it was a Guard stating that Michael had been involved in an accident over sixty miles away. An elderly cyclist who had an ash plant crosswise on his bicycle, had passed too near the car and was thrown heavily. This more or less put a damper on his tour, though none of the occupants of his car was hurt. The news was unnerving for the women but they decided not to worry. Madge forced Mrs Canning to pull on her coat after the meal and to go out and climb to a wooded place near the town. Terna had to answer Vane's last letter, so she fetched a writing pad and pen. It would do her good to write in the open. Outside, Madge wandered around for a while, and then Terna joined her, putting the *screed*, as Vane would have called it laughingly, into its envelope without closing it. Both of them were thoughtful. Away from the wooded scene, they stood to take in the irregular tract of poor pasture land where the grey remains of downy thistles and unsightly rushes were. In a mossy spot, wild flags without their golden heads were massed together to form a spreading clump. Then the walkers turned towards the road just as a white blade of late sun fell on them. And here they remained to inhale draught after draught of ice-clear air, until Terna felt the marsh wet through the soles of her fine shoes.

As they picked their steps daintily on the homeward path Terna's eyes fell on another patch of four and five-leafed clovers. As once before, she was inclined to pass it by but the girl thought the clovers were lucky and she took them home. Before post time that evening Terna added a postscript to Vane's letter, telling him of her find. And before a week had elapsed, Vane had replied in typically schoolboy parlance, 'that she must have been near a big plunge of good luck'. His mother corrected him for even entertaining such a thought. She was emphatically against it.

Peter rang to say that the injured man intended to follow for compensation and that their visitor would have to attend the court. She hoped fervently for a satisfactory settlement out of court and said so when Peter came home on his own, and Blitz remained with her uncle.

Terna was deeply concerned, when another guest came to cheer them. He was Peter's nephew, a student of Arts and Commerce in Dublin University who had been at the same college as Vane. The boy enlivened the place for a weekend. While in Cane Street he attended a dance in the hall right across the road where the band blared for hours. This was the usual thing on Friday nights in Glenmark during the dancing season ...

When the court case came off, the Judge ruled in Michael's favour, settling it in a few words and suggesting that the defendant put a donation in the poor box. Terna and Peter gave a joint offering in gratitude when Michael had to leave, with the intention of visiting Rome on the way back.

The same order held, homecomings and departures of the young people and others. Gay and Vane were making good headway when the big decision of Blitz's secondary school cropped up. Gay would be soon in her final year and then?

There was a beautifully situated Convent about two miles from Robinstown where Peter's sister lived in the County of Longford, and it was here that her parents installed Blitz on an early September day. The sun rose slowly that morning, and with less splendour. Though Terna's interest in the things of the moment kept her eyes from straying to the first drooping of garden flowers, she looked forward to travelling on the white roads for sixty miles while the light lasted. She knew the way well. Trees, shrubs and lawns would appear and disappear like mirrored, multiple images when they least expected. And where the tops of tall trees sunned themselves, a high breeze and dancing light would create an impression of open-work. And then Blitz's destination would shine through more trees and carefully kept spaces.

Blitz took in everything and Terna avoided telling her how they would miss her. Meeting the nuns and settling in came naturally to her, so much so, that she found nothing amiss in bursting into song before the nuns and boarders on her first evening when she should be studying the new programme. She loved singing at home, and also trying little airs for Terna's attempts at the lyrics.

Terna had then a new opening for more stories on ordinary themes, while Peter was considering studying for promotion, but changed his mind overnight about it, and Terna did not urge him. An amusing incident at that time was coming across a list of nicknames which Blitz had for Jay, some of them abbreviated: Jam, Jut, Jutty, Godlin, Jutteen, Gollilly, Golly, Gusty, Justy, Orduck, Babdeen, Raynor, Just, Ox, Little Man, Little Feller, Sticky, Stick, Butto, Jimmy, Fat Golly, Bubbie, Gol, Bubdeen, Nurtereen, Nuremburg, Golikus and Urtyburty.

Each name was written in an artistic hand as if the lot were worthy of perpetuity, a collection to be passed on or privately perused, and she signed it with an elaborate Blitz, and added a seraph. Such a collection! Off and on before, the family would hear Blitz repeat all the names to herself, but Terna never asked for an explanation. Blitz had an expansive imagination. 'Blitz should become an actress,' Terna would comment from time to time. Her daughter's apt descriptions of places and people since she left were most interesting, even about the smallest village on her way up.

She wrote before she left:

> I love my mother very much,
> She is handsome, she is holy.
> She has goldy hair like mine,
> And she leaves it goldy.

> She walks three miles each sunny day
> And then she rests,
> Does her household jobs
> And thanks for the worst and best.
> She's up as early as the birds
> To pray for the ones in Purgatory
> And she praises my little brother.

Blitz was in her element among books and scholars at all times, and was very attentive. Now the first account of her from the nuns was that she had got a hundred out of a hundred in Mathematics. All went very well there and she was proud of her teachers. She also visited her aunt regularly with a school pal whose father had gone to school in the east with her own father. That friend married a doctor later and went to live in Scotland for some time. Both Blitz and herself had much common and also much general information.

Then Blitz started to lose her appetite and did not look forward to her meals at all. 'Ah! every hill must have its hollow,' her mother told Peter. 'Look at this!' It was the Summer vacation. Tempting and coaxing were to no avail, and finally, Terna spoke to a doctor and he advised a change of school, and Terna acted on it. She applied to a Benedictine Order of nuns in a beautiful, remote part of the West of Ireland, enquiring if they had a place. The answer was prompt and favourable, so Terna went to Kylemore to express her pleasure and her thanks. The first meeting with the Reverend Mother Prioress was easy and natural and Terna noted the strength of character in the nun's face. Chatting inside after, the nun was pleased with the detailed description of Blitz, of her independent nature and her wish to find out everything for herself, and to make her own decisions. And Blitz? She jumped with joy when her mother informed her of the results. It had to be seen to be believed as time passed: the transformation in that worthy girl! Were attitudes, conditions, air and approach so important that they constituted such a change? Where the Abbey is situated is just an artist's dream, a very beautiful, mountainous stretch, abounding in rocks and retreats where saints would love to pray and poets compose. It has all the sequestration and green, unfrequented paths that a solitary nature loves. Not that Blitz was a solitary, she was out-going.

Some people say things casually that often turn out to be pointers to be remembered and regretted. A certain nun saw Blitz walk past one day and she remarked to somebody *that Blitz might not be so long for this world*. Terna was unmoved at that and soon forgot all about it for the newly-revitalised girl was on the road to up and up.

Next, Terna accepted an invitation to South Galway. Everything and everybody there were much the same, with the exception of Jock whose doctor had ordered an operation for the removal of ulcers. It was a critical and trying time for him and Fay until the day he came home. For weeks after, he went on a light diet and slowly regained his appetite for solid food. So hard work was out of the question for him for the rest of the time. 'Well and good,' said Fay.

Terna was barely at home when Jay rang from Cratton to say that his wife had just died in the Dublin hospital, which meant that the Cannings would meet the funeral on its way to Cratton. Oh! it was so pathetic to see the young children peep into their mother's coffin before it was closed. Jay himself was like a figure cut out of stone, though he confided to Terna that release was better than to have his wife suffer any longer. Babe was at the stage of her illness when she questioned rebelliously – the unfairness of it all. It was a sad and bleak situation for him, but he faced his widowerhood manfully, and found a father's joy in his children, and in educating them. He never remarried.

A new practice in Cannings was that the children away at school should spend part of each vacation at a relative's home. So Vane stepped off the train at the end of his next term on his way from the South and spent nearly a fortnight with his lonely uncle, Jay. Vane kept his family fully informed of every change there, every happening and of almost every thought in his head. Gay was already in her last year and her mind had been made up, for the family intended to spend a holiday by the sea that year.

The letters of school activities were good. Vane had won another Question Time and had written a short poem for his college Annual. Gay's final examination over, she started a commercial course in Dublin for a Bank post which was within her reach. But her parents would have preferred her to go to the University. Eventually, she did neither, but took up secretarial work in the Ministry of Defence, in England, in due course. And before she started, the family went to a famous holiday venue in the south of Ireland.

# CHAPTER 21

# Fears and Hopes

When Vane was home again, he prepared Jay for his confirmation. And on the big day Jay was asked a Bible story and a parable. Jay had been serving Mass for a few years and the time leading up to his Primary tests. He proudly purchased an expensive world atlas from his pocket money and ran to show it to his mother who refunded some of the cost. His gesture was heartening.

A most relaxing period followed for Peter and Terna. Life was good in its essence, without a material surfeit. Most of their initial planning for their children was almost over. So Terna tackled the house with Madge. The bedrooms were looking tired, and she shopped for hours until her ankles ached, to get the exact shades she wanted. She finally decided on powder blue, lavender and greeny-blue for she had quilts and bedcovers in mixed shades of those. Peter remarked that the place had the appearance of a Grade A hotel when finished inside. He shed all his officialdom while he worked in dungarees applying the oil paint, then he took over the outside with the help of a younger man. The house had been a dull grey that looked twice as dull on dark days. After the work was finished with a slaty colour at the base and above, the building appeared twice as large. The front door was flaking and a coat of paint improved it. Then Terna added bright containers of flowers and small shrubs, mostly subjects that would perish if left to the ravages of frost in the garden.

When the walls were finished, all the doors were painted white inside, and as that colour would not be practical for outside on account of the dust, dashes from traffic and drips from the eave shoots, a petrol blue was considered more suitable for them. Opposite the house in front was a vacant, weedy plot. It had been part of a wide field formerly. Someone had purchased the site, intending to build on it but failed to do so. Unpruned, overhanging trees were unsightly, and spreading roots of wild shrubs, elder and briar had increased. A rickety, rusty gate divided the rural patch from Cane Street and even part of the former was covered with tangled growth from post to post. When the loudest winds of the year finally came and launched an attack on the rural eyesore, thousands of leaves rose and rested in long piles at the side of the Cannings' house. The place was literally littered with those foot-stalks and peduncles of flowers of many florets, after their short span from the tender foliage stage to their first discolouration and ultimate death. The plot had a roughly-erected wall all round with one side lower than the others, near where the winds played a requiem of their own regularly among the drooping branches. Terna usually became deeply absorbed in it, but Peter hated the finality of it all.

Ever from her youngest day Terna respected grass and greenery. She ascribed a certain power to them in their verdant, perennial softness, the power of renewal. Her rural explorations were good for the spirit at all times. It was on one of those turns that she felt that Gay and herself should go on foot to Knock Shrine. The fact that Blitz had been cured there had endeared the place to them. And Gay did not hesitate for a moment. She was very vigorous, and Terna was equal to the journey. They did not look on it as a challenge. So, on Gay's next stay they both retired very early and began their slow journey at 5.15 a.m., carrying nothing except rosaries and the barest amount to eat, a few oranges to revive them. Leaving the silent house and the sleeping town behind them they noticed semi-circular fingers of light above the horizon which would develop into streaks as daylight crept over the dim scenes before them. An ancient grey castle dominated the few houses near it. It was more distinct than they were. Odd pale stars showed and disappeared, but two large ones that remained were as fixed as a lighthouse. Not the time for twittering yet, so the hedges along the way rested in their green, free from the hopping and darting of their feathered burdens.

As the mother and daughter advanced, Terna moved like a creature of air and Gay an agile ground bird. Terna had a kind of jealous joy at the undertaking, knowing that there would be no second time. They were approaching the little village of Ganacloy, their first on the hilly road. They were unbelievably fresh and quickened their pace. It was only a matter of growing used to walking, and the pedestrian pilgrims refrained from speaking much so as to keep their thoughts on their holy goal.

By then the fingers of light had gone, and the golden crown of the sun had moved up, and was throwing its beams over a slowly wakening world. Oh! the silence and the magic of the period between the dawn and day, and the signs of life that followed one another, all going forward convenient ... to the advantage of different species.

On arrival at Irishtown a larger village with a beautiful church, the women saw smoke in broken, sooty whiffs from puffing chimneys. Not a bone or an ankle ached, not even when they had arrived in Ballindine, a small place of one street, of solid homes and open countryside around. Both Irishtown and Ballindine were in the County of Mayo. Terna and Gay made no delay in either place, and for the first time since they stepped on those major roads that lead to Knock, a ferocious Alsatian rushed out from a private entrance and almost tore them to pieces. Only Gay had the presence of mind to stoop as if she were picking up a stone and then approached the animal fearlessly; the vicious attacker would not have withdrawn before he savaged them. Terna's distant patting and petting would not have been of any use at all. They stood, and after much glaring and many growls, the dog turned towards the house.

The women were safe and they went their way, Terna glancing backwards apprehensively until they were out of sight of the house. Birdsong all around made them lessen their pace, for it started in a sudden gush, and the piping went on with double and treble notes until the morning was filled with melody of a pervasive wind.

'This is all too beautiful, don't lose a detail of it,' Terna said. 'It's for storing in the mind, Gay!'

'It's worth remembering, indeed.' Gay agreed.

'Too many people are both blind and deaf to the simple sights and sounds which are meant to gladden us, country treats. Worldly acquisition alone cannot be all that satisfying to the section of creation which is supposed to possess a spark of the divine,' Terna added. 'Men should neither be slaves nor masters of economy only.'

'There is so much in what you say, Mammy!'

They walked along, never even consulting their watches until they sighted the Castle McGarret wood and rhododendrons. Further than to admire the place and the lay-out, they had not any interest in it, so they pushed on, still regaled by the hedge artistes. At a turning, a shallow river came into view where over a dozen white gulls looked as if they were stationary there. Then the silent pilgrims shared an orange for instant energy and plodded on regardless of the fatigue that, nevertheless, was setting in on both. By the time they had reached a town over twice as large as Glenmark, a place called Claremorris, they were tempted to order lunch but their pilgrim spirit got the upper hand, so they rested only for a short time and continued on their way. On and on while Terna imagined that she had been borne along until they found themselves on the actual spot of the heavenly Apparitions where Terna knew that there was telepathic energy between Vane and herself. She was to pray hardest for him. There they performed like other pilgrims, rested for a short time again, and then finally retraced their steps to the house in Cane Street. On the return journey, step by step became more painful and it took an hour longer. Though Gay was equal to it, the fact that they still observed their fast from solids proved too much for her mother and delayed her. So time ticked away and darkness fell and increased to the folds of night, but this was the one occasion on which Terna was not *moved* to describe it. And at 1 a.m. after some twenty hours in all and forty-two miles later, they dragged themselves to a table to eat before they finally lay down in their beds in Glenmark.

What had Peter been thinking of as he hopped in and out of the house? From 8 p.m. he could not relax or eat. He thought of the different turns on a strange road of accidents. He considered sending a car for them, but he did not know which route they took. He waited, and went to bed later than usual, not to sleep for he was tense, staring, imagining ... and began to breathe evenly only when he heard their steps below.

A pilgrimage is a pilgrimage. It must entail suffering. Not until next morning did Terna really feel the blisters on her heels and toes, wide, red patches of broken skin, raw and bare. She understood then, and only then, why the sheets had irritated her when she stretched, and why she had had to shift from one position to the other before she slept. She had to apply a cream and peroxide and heal them. And further, her calves refused to function. They were as stiff as boards from the strain and her bodily structure seemed to be out of joint. She even found it difficult to sit up in bed, so she had to remain in a recumbent position for almost three days. As for Gay, she was up and about the next morning and ready for action in the afternoon.

All things considered, the Cannings had much to be thankful for. Whenever a niggling worry would arise, they would not entertain it. Each day was a lifelet to be lived to the full. They understood that one gets out of life what one puts into it, another kind of investment ...

Vane never forgot a promise as far as his mother was concerned. He walked in one evening with another kitten creeping all over him and it wheezing weakly as he landed it on Terna's lap to be fondled.

'Vane! how nice,' she cried. 'Where did you find it? Raise it?'

'In the country. Blitz has mentioned something about calling the next pet Faust,' and Faust it was. Terna had secretly intended to buy a small dog but she did not say as much to Vane for it would spoil the moment for him. She began to break in the new addition to the family immediately by feeding it first, closing the doors and encouraging it to lie on a basket. Coaxing was necessary right from the start for the kitten was fond of its own way, if not a little heedless, Terna concluded, when compared with the last one. The coming weeks showed an improvement in their friend and its owners could forget about her sometimes and have a day off.

CHAPTER 22

# Treats and Illness

But Terna had a certain sense of incompleteness, for her old urge for a canine pal surged back constantly. And in a matter of months when Faust was hardy enough to stay out on her own, Terna's eye fell on the dog column of *the Independent*, and after scanning the advertisements she found what she fancied, a Pembroke corgi for sale. It was a box number. She wrote for details and had them in a week. Out of the whole world, who should own the corgi but cousins of her husband in the County Longford. Terna had met them once before, after her honeymoon when they extended & warm invitation to Peter and herself. When the family discovered who the buyers were, the mother asked them to bring or send for the dog, a puppy of seven weeks. So Peter contacted a friend who used to pass by the seller's place a few times a week and who had no objection to oblige him. And so the corgi with the fine, fawn coat as smooth as ermine, was handed in at the Barracks in Glenmark in a matter of days. Peter happened to be Barrack Orderly the same day and he had to hold the splendid animal until he returned to tea. Then Luxo, for Terna had named him the instant she saw him, made himself at home at once. Terna was charmed with him every way, especially that he was a watchdog and good with friends. Though regretfully, man's best friend took a ready dislike to his kind master, and only appeared civil when taken for a walk by him. The relationship was one thing that Terna could not change. She regretted the new pet's gritting of teeth and his growls as soon as Peter would remove the lead after a country tramp.

Terna loved Luxo from the start and he was easy to teach. As he grew older he took a special delight in minding the garden for her.

102

Even passing birds soon learned that they could not alight, and stray cats fled at the sight of him. And often he tumbled down the steps leading from the garden, his healthy, roly-poly body panting after racing round and barking his lungs out. There was one cat that did not fear him, Faust, that stood up to him with arching independence. At length the two agreed to agree. After scampering off from him a few times, Faust approached him, purring, and so the truce was signed. When Luxo became strong and too energetic, it was impossible to get him to bed. So Terna wrote a little stanza for him to no particular air, and sang him to sleep:

> *Off to sleep, good Luxo,*
> *Close your hazel eyes.*
> *Off to sleep, good Luxo,*
> *It's time to say goodnight.*
> *Off to sleep, good Luxo,*
> *To dream all on your own*
> *All good doggies like you*
> *Do what they are told.*

The oddest thing that the Cannings noticed was that Luxo picked out one of the many hen trespassers in the garden, and made a pet of her. They lay in the sun, the corgi half curled round her. That was it for the most of a year, until the feathered friend was no longer a good layer, and her owner sold her. Luxo never took on another hen friend. Terna valued her royal pet so much that he was never allowed on the street unaccompanied or without a lead with his name on it. Peter feared for him.

While Gay was succeeding at her chosen work, the oldest sister of the Cannings put in an appearance again, looking like sweet sixteen. With her was a cousin who was now suffering from a heart condition. They entered a discussion about Jay's leaving the National School. Jay would not hear of going far away to college. He begged his parents to let him attend a day school, and he promised to study hard. After what amounted to a round-the-table conference both parents eventually agreed that he could go to the Christian Brothers in a town eight miles away. Unfortunately, the boy fell ill and Terna thought it advisable that he should attend the Glenmark National School for another year. He was very young and could afford to do without it as yet. Poor Jay was a home lover always and would even cut short a day's outing to be back in Glenmark with his parents. He loved to go to sporting fixtures.

The visitors next left on a tour of Ireland to call on the many friends of her friends in America who were Irish and of Irish descent. With the children away at school, their parents planned outings as they missed their brightness, songs and their generally entertaining manner. Television and radio were poor substitutes for their laughing exchanges.

Jay was deeply interested in his books by then, and his parents knew just how they stood. Terna was not mad for dressing up and attending parties every night of the week, for she found pen work a blessing altogether. Her adult mind learned to be content with what came, the sweet and bitter uncertainties and certainties of life.

The news was interesting some time after. Gay had received a proposal of marriage from a landowner which she turned down on the grounds that she preferred her post. Terna disliked the idea of her daughter emigrating but Gay felt it was for the best. And Gay made very good friends there who had her interests at heart. A lady who had become a friend constantly reminded her of the perils awaiting young girls in a new country. Gay suffered minor indispositions at first, but grew used to climatic conditions. Blitz and herself corresponded regularly, making happy references to good times and pranks of the past, and with a list of plans for the future. The two valued sisterly companionship.

Further partings were on. Terna had to break it kindly to Madge that she could dispense with her services, and Madge readily understood. So Peter placed the girl in the country with a couple who had four young children. She married later in the country. Madge's going left Terna less time for meditating and committing her thoughts to paper. It was stalemate. Peter described it as starting all over again in Glenmark, a new course in adaptability.

Some of the older furniture was beginning to look shabby and out of place, so once she packed the fridge for Peter and Jay, and departed to Dublin to order modern sitting room furniture. She remained a night away and travelled home with the driver who delivered the suite. The upholstered pieces matched the hangings and the carpet which did not appear old and faded against them. But there was something missing. As most of the glassware had been on the sideboard since they opened house she decided to have a glass case at last. It had a cocktail section at the base without glass. It was mahogany and worth every penny it cost. Terna kept the silver on one side. It was a sight to gladden a woman's heart, when the Waterford glass caught the beams of sunny light from the window opposite. All comers admired it until they grew used to it, and then they said nothing at all; it was no longer a topic of interest.

The family was to have their lives punctuated with regrettable events, and it was Jock's chronic illness then that sprang up. Most of his stomach had to be cut away. He hardly ever grew hungry then, and after some months he had wasted to a mere skeleton with a cadaverous colour. Following all the operations, weakness set in so he could no longer manage the farm work. But Fay hoped for the best with all the care and treatment.

Jock had been an early riser all his life, seven o'clock never saw him in bed. His collies and cattle dogs were always at the ready, they knew their master's ways so well. The farmers around never needed to look at a clock, for the short, sharp barks of the dogs broke upon the morning regularly, to be followed, occasionally, by Jock's imperative whistles. Imagine those shrilly noises cutting through the sleepy air over walled gardens and sheltered fields, and from animals being counted and examined by a serious farmer's eye. An attack known as 'staggers' in the sheep was troublesome off and on. Jock believed in milking cows twice a day, and he kept eighteen of them so shortage of milk was unheard of. Jock was then forced to pay a farm hand. His children were too young to take on heavy jobs. He found the idleness that was thrust on him boring in the extreme and Fay made a special effort to cheer him. Early foddering on an empty stomach with a rushed, late breakfast of fried food, had been mostly responsible for his breakdown in health, first. But what he loved he ate.

Terna was on the spot when Fay needed her, but she could not do the impossible, and Jock became discouraged after nearly a year of half starvation. He began to attend the doctors again but had not the same interest in going. Fay looked on, hoping for a better day while great circles showed under her eyes and she hid her tears.

Then Peter offered to come at weekends to help the workman, while Vena showed up to manage the children when she could. And when Terna threw herself into manual work she watched that her mind did not stagnate. She made time to concentrate on the beautiful by eye, ear and mind, without making beauty a cult. So despite the abrupt changes, she preserved an enviable inner peace. Though that inner peace was soon to be shattered by his college doctor informing her that Vane would have to be operated on. So in the first few days of his next holiday his parents saw to everything. He had got a blow from a hurley on the knee and it had made a bad gathering which had to be removed to spare possible amputation of the limb.

Once again, Vane was lucky, and for a year after he had to exercise the limb until it was flexible again. Terna hated his colour and she treated him to the best tonics and nourishment. As in Jock's case, she had now a depressed boy on her hands, though he was never difficult.

Blitz and Terna planned little getaways when Vane had improved sufficiently to play games and walk again. Mother and daughter once toured the South-West of Ireland, where they became acquainted with reporters, literary people and editors. After the short tour, Terna wrote two compositions: *Abbeyleix* and *Garden of Dreams*, both of which were to appear in the newspapers, *the Leinster Times* and the *Kilkenny People*. The opening of the first song went like this:

> *If an angel grew tired of his glory above*
> *And would rest in this world for a while,*
> *He would fly to the Laoisland and there fall in love*
> *And stay to the end of all time.*

The second song is *Garden of Dreams*:

> *In my heart there's a garden of beautiful dreams*
> *Where bluebirds are singing a song, etc.*

The most prosaic would have to speak about the scenery of that part of Ireland. The rich lands gave an expansive appearance to the different areas. Fine roads ran between the green plains and tillage fields. Lordly trees saluted the sun, rising or setting, on its course from east to west, and birds hid and hopped with rousing diapason where the women walked.

Blitz was anxious to go further but their time was limited and she was studying hard for an examination at the time. A week-end would have to do, though Vane had rung to say he was feeling fine. And Gay was coming to the Isle of Man to meet Blitz there, if possible. Besides, a German friend of a nun had extended an invitation to her whenever she could come.

Terna was back in Cane Street busily engaged when Peter announced at lunch that he had been to the doctor about his back. 'Your back?' His wife put a towel away. 'I never knew.'

'The doctor says that I have a slipped disc.'

'But you had no pain, you never complained.'

'Only this morning in the dayroom.'

'Heavens! Have you been lifting anything heavy?'

'Not since carrying in the new furniture and changing out the old, you remember.' He frowned slightly. 'And lifting it on the van when we sold it.'

Her eyes widened then. 'Oh! Peter!' She was genuinely concerned. 'Wha ... what else did the doctor say? Tell me.'

'He is sending me to the Depot hospital in Dublin for treatment.' She turned aside.

'Have courage, he said, it is not a killer disease, just the lumber disc out of place.'

The journey to the hospital took three hours, and by the time Peter was receiving treatment at the hands of a physiotherapist Terna was somewhat relieved. She summoned all her powers of endurance then for she wished to keep her faith shining. Peter was strapped in a hard material from foot to head for two hours every day for a few weeks, face downwards, under ultra violet light. Terna was told that he would be possibly six weeks in hospital to effect a cure. Peter was a good patient.

'I suppose I have to suffer now for being so proud of the furniture, and all of you, Jay!' she sighed.

'That has nothing to do with it, Mammie! Do not be blaming yourself. Those things happen, and Dad is in the right hands.'

She grew cheerful then and sent Jay to make another phone call to the Depot. Every ring confirmed an improvement in his father's condition and Terna sat back to see the soul of good in the whole thing. Peter would benefit from the change, anyway, and he had an opportunity to call on his aging brother. When next Terna called to see him she was happy to see the improvements in him, even in his stance.

It is amazing how strain can affect the whole body, especially when one is standing or active. Peter's favourite fruit and books were packed and posted, unless delivered by hand. He had read *the Argosy* for years.

Then, at another weekend, Terna and Blitz climbed the Holy

107

mountain, Croagh Patrick near Westport. That kind of hurt did no harm to anybody, Terna held, and maybe good for somebody else. Blitz was not as robust as Gay, so the climb was slow and the effort arduous, often a step on and a step back. The ascent took four-and-a-half hours and the descent was much easier. At times, Terna wondered if her second son had been right when he advised them against it. It was worth it all and the mother kept Blitz home for a day longer and served all her meals in bed. The nuns were very sympathetic in all the ups and downs of Blitz's people.

Though Terna made a few more trips to Dublin, her mind was just as occupied with thoughts of Vane for he had just won a gold medal for Debate. At the same time thoughts of a religious vocation were dawning on him, and he referred to this briefly in a letter. But it transpired in a later letter to Terna that he was anxiously looking forward to coming home for he had been very run down all that term and had kept the fact from his parents.

'So far, so good, so far, so bad,' she said, and left it at that for the time being. Vane in his last year in college! All the family would be home for their father's return and then the plans would be set afoot, she reckoned, not wishing to be pessimistic at that moment.

# CHAPTER 23

# *Facing Up To It*

After his treatment Peter arrived home in good fettle. His back was not exactly perfect, but a month later, as he sat up in bed, he felt something loosen in his spine, and he called Terna to tell her that the disc had gone back into place. It was goodbye to his lumbar trouble, but she persuaded him to keep a recumbent position for hours after, and on each day until he was fit for duty again. The official was such a change. Another change: the nephew who visited before had then graduated and was marrying a Dublin girl, another graduate. Peter attended the wedding. The venue of the honeymoon was a secret.

An evening by the sea followed for the family. Vane seemed in good form, and Blitz had to leave them for the date of her German visit was near and as she had set her heart on learning German, she grasped the opportunity of hearing it spoken by natives, the best way to learn a language.

Coming and going was most enjoyable, but before long, Vane was giving cause for anxiety. He fell very silent on occasions and answered laconically. Peter felt the change in his eldest son deeply, for it was quite clear that Vane was suffering from *nerves*.

'Surely, Peter, life for us is no grand illusion. Is everything to go by the wall for us? Are we to be pursued with the sudden and the sad? Just when your back is better. If the sun shines on us for a day we have to be penalized for it.'

'We will not look at it that way, Terna!' She paced.

'No wonder I was apprehensive. Poor Vane will hardly get his wish, to have his bones bleached on the mission fields after helping to save souls for most of his life.'

'That is a bit far-fetched. And people fall ill and grow well again.'

'Maybe,' she said, and she went to Vane to try to make him speak to her. But his vacant eyes told her everything. With a kind of desperate courage she drew him away, showing him the prizes he had won and reading his debate in the college Annual, when Vane made a wild dash for the garden and would not come back for a meal. Then his mood changed to aggressiveness and he shook from head to foot. He refused the medicine that the local doctor had mixed for him, and by next evening Vane had been placed under the doctors. He did not know where he was. On the way home, neither Peter nor Terna could get a word to say. At home the father whispered that time was a healer for everything. He did not despair fully, and by the next day Terna's frame of mind was a little better. Vane incapacitated ... for how long?

The parents travelled the thirty-two miles to the hospital next day, only to find Vane with the same vacant look from suspended reasoning. He had to be led to the table and to bed, and was having his first electric shock next day. Vane's father and mother had to give permission for the treatment. They ate or drank little on the journey. Jay was comfort itself but anything he would say fell on deaf ears.

'You are a woman who keeps faith,' he said over and over again, 'do not forget.' And that started Terna thinking again.

Vane and herself had had two long holidays together in their lives. Then the day she thought that she had lost him sailed back into mind, and his manly, intelligent way telling her how he stole off to see the old boat and his regretting its condition after a long time on the waters! Jay missed his brother so much that he remained sleepless at night for weeks and his studies suffered.

Breaking the news of Vane's illness to Gay and Blitz fell to Terna. She began by saying that as Vane had been in poor health for some time, and rather than wait to see him break up seriously, they took safety measures for his sake. The sisters were sorrowful. In a short time Gay gave up her secretarial work and learned nursing so that she could eventually mind Vane and even *cure* him. Her heart was in her work. 'Some of the finest specimens of humanity alienated and wasted,' she grieved. Peter was glad that Vane was alive, anyway, and he tried to bring Terna around to his way of thinking.

'I suppose we are going to be spiritualised with sorrow, and that is all about it,' she breathed.

When they were growing resigned and visiting Vane regularly, the kind Uncle Michael flew home to see his favourite nephew to whom he meant to leave a business, and Vane being mission-minded, had changed all that before. Gay arrived unexpectedly while Michael was home, and she was a power of consolation to them. She had seen so much illness that she convinced her parents that Vane's case was not a cause for despair at all. A slight nervous disorder was all she could make of it, for Vane had not lost his sense of direction at all and she had succeeded in squeezing a few words from him. Nobody was in the humour for driving around that time, and the visitors enjoyed the house comforts that Peter and Terna offered in such a whole-hearted way.

When the goodbyes were said at the end with assurances of another visit, when possible, from those two, the natural philanthropist and 'the sweet lady' – Terna Canning, Terna of Carfort, undertook bout after bout of manual work in an attempt to wean herself, even momentarily, from pressing thoughts.

It was evening by the time she finished on a certain day at the beginning of the next week as she had worked strenuously from an early hour between house and garden while her husband was on relief duty. And when the last gleams of daylight melted into night, she *waited*, *waited*, and then sought the sanctuary of the darkness in the garden in Glenmark. This time it was only a little different to the moment when she had taken her first step into the darkness as a pedestrian pilgrim on the Knock–Glenmark road. She moved closer to the huge tree and then, suddenly, the noon sun that often lit up the interior of her late brother's room was dim, distant, next to the flash of inspiration that she received, lost in the deepest waves of darkness, where no echoes could penetrate. Turning in, she mentally repeated the remainder of the composition for Michael, and when she had penned it, she wrote about the mountain streams in South Galway – the slow streams of Killcross. The lyric had two verses. They have not been set to music, so far, and may never be.

As can be understood, Terna knew a real relief when she laid down her pen and began to ready herself for a well-earned rest. It was late when she was surprised by a lady whom she barely knew, carrying a bundle of magazines. She was the type who usually talked best after midnight when she could: and she had a strong voice with an elastic tongue and most of her sayings started with 'I' stressed.

111

'*I* thought you'd like these,' she began, as she threw the books on a side table. 'You're great for ideas, yourself.' She sniggered. 'It tightens me to write a letter, *I* tell you. If *I* leave it until night *I*'m done!'

'Is that the way?' Terna managed to say.

The uninvited guest went on as if she were her own audience.

'*I* never thought of the time.'

'It is all right, I do not mind,' her listener covered up.

'Look at that,' the woman shouted, 'you're goin' round it like a lady. An' you could be ragin' inside.'

'I am not, not at all. There should be time for everybody. Time is not that precious.'

'Thanks, Ma'am!' She looked embarrassed then and sat sideways on a chair in a drab frock frayed at the hem from rubbing against her powerful legs.

'You know there's an old lady who calls you the makin' of a martyr?' Terna nodded. 'Well, she's killed prayin' for your son, and so am *I*.'

She changed her position and Terna caught the scent of cheap perfume; the woman believed in a regular sprinkle rather than a daily wash.

'That is good for you both.'

'Seems some have to suffer and others go free in this world.'

'It – it – is – so. That is just it.'

'Ah! but you've a power of courage,' she paused. 'And *I* suppose you'd rather if *I* called it fortitude when you're one for describin' properly.'

'What difference? We are being tried with this cross and we will go on with it.'

'The way you look at it! If it were *me*, *I*'d damn and blast and strike out against it. An' by the way, how's himself takin' it?'

'Well, he would rather if it had not happened, but we share the trouble and that lightens it a little for the time being.' She rose to get a drink, but the older woman thanked her and moved to the door.

'*I* never touch it, Mrs Canning, not a drop. *I*'ll be goin' now, and if I could do anything, *I*'d do it. I would then. Goodnight now to you!'

'Goodnight, and thanks for the books,' said Terna, as she left her to the door and then turned back, smiling.

'Such a rough-spoken, well-meaning creature, and a rather egoistic one!'

She went to the bottom of the stairs and searched for the switch, and as she did so, Peter walked in as the door was ajar. His coming was a happy interruption.

'We've had a visitor, or sympathiser, Peter! All about Vane.'

'Oh! Who?'

'I am not sure of her name, honestly I am not. I know her to see.' She prepared a very late supper and forgot about sleep until her husband had eaten and she had glanced over the magazines, page by page.

'They seem to look on sick people as victims of creation, around here,' she whispered.

'Often looks like it, Terna, but time does not stand still and hope springs always,' he smiled. After that they retired, Terna determined to put a gnawing awareness of their new stroke out of her mind for a few hours.

The next morning Terna was up and doing earlier than what she expected. After the extra exertion of the day before she had not to resort to drugs or drink to induce sleep. When the breakfast rashers, sausages and eggs were frying on the cooker she heard a rush of animal feet in the garden and made her way to where Luxo was engaged pulling a half dead crow to pieces. She freed the bird and left him for Peter to handle, at the same time driving the dog into the house.

Then she took in the morning. As far as her eye could travel the quiet scenes seemed to have a soul of their own. At her feet lay spent plants without a whiff of their former fragrance, some of then beaten flat with the chubby feet of Luxo, the corgi. And then, as if acting as purifiers before the veil of morning was fully lifted, silver rain fell in scattered drops. Before she left she looked in the direction of Vane's hospital.

Peter was downstairs when she returned a few minutes after to serve breakfast. When they were seated, they discussed the new move in the family, Blitz's going to the University of Galway to read Arts, Commerce and the Higher Diploma in Education. At vacation time she travelled much, both at home and abroad. Her horizons were widening year after year until she finally graduated with honours. She included French in her academic course, though she had never learnt any in her secondary school. Her next degree was a Master of Arts, in German through Irish, which was to be followed by a Law Course,

113

some of which took place in Gray's Inns, Dublin. Blitz had succeeded at everything she undertook. So did Jay that year for he passed his Intermediate examination with honours. In his case there was cause for satisfaction, listening to his teachers speak of him.

Blitz went to Scotland and the Lake District at her next opportunity and gave full details to her people. And whether on holiday tours or studying, books were her constant companions. Some years later it was said that her car was like a mobile library at all times. Travel, cultural attainments and acquiring knowledge were the be-all and end-all of her life. By this time she was more robust and agile than when growing up. Peter was proud of her, as were her uncles and aunts, but never as proud as Terna had been of Vane, no matter what circumstances. In his ruined state she saw an underlying betterment, but when? She feared that sorrow would jolt her into indifference if she allowed it. She had seen one of her nearest relatives in the world, part of whose life was a long lapse of partial despair.

And into this time of brave striving came Michael again, when she had to dress to go to a race meeting with Peter and him, where she picked and backed winners, though mechanically. Michael had aged and his hair was white.

In a hotel later, Terna's only snatches of her old humour returned, for she was with Vane, the shut-in, in that old, grey group of buildings. When they were passing out she saw bottles of Coca-Cola in a row, Vane's favourite and only drink. Outside at last, they entered an opposite shop holding a wool jacket the same style Vane was wearing in his last term in college. Reminders, none of them refreshing, of her wasted son!

The ever dependable Michael stayed a week when they aimed at being nominally happy, helping each other to bear up. They started on a Saturday morning and drove all through West Galway and round the coast. They dined at the best places on the way and took long walks. The walking was Michael's idea for an uplifting of the spirits. They had gone that way before and knew what to expect. Peter loved the trip. He got time off for he had relieved other Garda friends often. And on the last three days in Cane Street Michael was to be informed of something that would amount to a problem for all; Jay had confided to him that he would not go back to school any more.

Time was short, but his uncle used it to coax, lead or persuade his nephew to consider what he said and to count the possible consequences. Michael summoned his parents and acquainted them of his decision. Peter was angry and disappointed, so disappointed that he did not say what he would have liked to say just then. Terna remarked: 'It cannot be true,' pausing and growing incredulous, 'and if it is there must be a remedy.' She spoke kindly to Jay after which his father addressed him.

'It is hardly the way to do things, Son!'

Jay hated to stir up the paternal ire.

'I hate school, Dad!'

'What can you be without it?'

'I shall make out, do not fear,' Jay held.

After much pushing, Peter gave in.

Terna was amazed at the turn her son had taken as he was kind and co-operative by nature and learning came so easily to him at all times. Not that Jay could be an idle boy; he hated inactivity. It moved his mother so much to see him so willing to help in a special way from morning until night, and yet neglect the main thing in life, a foothold, a security against its hazards.

Jay's uncle was truly disillusioned and made endless promises to him to win him over for his own good. It was useless, and as Michael's jet touched down at Idlewild Airport, he was asking himself what was to become of Jay Canning? Peter and Terna tried to make Jay see his mistake and by the end of a week Terna called off trying. She required more than a shining faith to keep looking straight. At this period and long before, Jay could have been referred to as a soccer fiend. So his mother jumped at the opportunity to suggest a college where the game was very popular. At this point, the boy became rather emotional.

'I am a disappointment to you, Mammy, but the only thing I want to do is to write a book about soccer. I could start it in the morning.'

'Jay! you must have more at your back than that. It could be only a sideline for one of your intelligence. It would not mean total and lasting satisfaction to you socially or from the point of view of self respect.'

Jay was silent for the whole day, and knew that his mother was aching to help him. 'I'll succeed sometime,' he said in a low voice, and the subject was closed.

'Trials, trials, not soul-splitting ones, I hope,' the woman of faith prayed. She took up her pen. 'Poor chips of the human circle, facing up to the angles and triangles of living,' she cried, and went out.

CHAPTER 24

# *Correspondence*

Terna was not a good correspondent when it came to writing letters, but she loved receiving them. During Michael's stay and the recent vicissitudes, a mass of work piled up. Letters from Gay and Blitz teemed with happy incidents of their daily lives. Gay wrote quite impressively of the men who had proposed marriage to her, of her new clothes, of the places she had visited and the friends that she had made. Vane got a whole page in her letters, the last one, and she always finished on a note of trust her brother would grow well. Blitz's missives were amusing, interesting, direct and to the point. Above any human being who ever walked the earth, Blitz Canning must have had an innate disgust for the processes of courtship and marriage. While friendship was sacred to her, she abhorred closer relationships. Whenever a hopeful suitor expressed himself with a view to marriage Blitz would ask, almost scream: 'Is it going to escalate to that?'

There was an inventor of a part of the computer whom she respected; over a dozen men of different callings who proposed to her after the first introduction and who suited her mentally; and other numerous hopefuls who had to go their way, hopeless. The longest attachment on a friendly basis was with a Professor's son whom she had met in the Galway University. That on and off friendship lasted a few years, more out of gratitude for his many kindnesses than anything else. Sometimes, mere acquaintances of hers would write to her mother to show them how to win her daughter.

'Marriage is not for everybody,' Blitz would shrug. She was married to books.

In the face of Vane's illness and Jay's refusal to study any more,

Terna was bound to lose some of her tone. So, on Blitz's return home she came to the rescue by taking her mother on a short motoring tour of the north east of their own country. Terna had just bought a very becoming suit in lemon and brown mixtures. The day before they began the run, Terna received a most surprising letter from a pal of her early school days, who very rarely wrote. The sender of the letter was full of praise for what Terna was like in Suntry school. Terna doubted if she deserved so much of a good thing, though her old pal could not flatter if she tried.

Mother and daughter went in the direction of Ballyhaunis, the town of the river under seven miles from Knock. From there they followed the busy roads leading to other Mayo towns, Charleston, Swinford, Balla, Foxford, Ballinrobe, Partry, Newport, Crossmolina, Westport, Killalla, Castlebar and wild Belmullet. North Mayo had the most rugged scenery. Changing direction, they found themselves in Charlestown once again. From there they went to Tubbercurry, a distance of seven miles, on to Grange, Curry, Ballisodare, Coloney and finally Sligo, where they stayed a night, in the Silver Swan Hotel. They had another look about in the morning before they drove to Ballyshannon, Bundoran and Ballintra, and later to Convoy, Moville, Donegal and Letterkenny (off route to Derry city).

It was at the start of the Northern Troubles there, and already kiosks were overturned, and buildings wrecked or burnt down with bombs. Only a place called the Diamond, the main business centre, was, so far, untouched, while panic-stricken assistants helped them choose. On account of the way things were in that city, most of the drapers had shelves of stuff on their hands as their usual set of customers remained away from possible danger, and dealt elsewhere. While there, Terna asked one question: How did the guerillas expect to end the agony and arrive at a peaceful conclusion if they intended to remain guerillas? Already, she had titled a poem: *Where peace lies.*

All the family received postcards from the absent ones and the senders sadly realized that Vane should never mention that he received any at all. The motorists had their car searched by police at different routes along the way.

Terna and Blitz returned at midday on the Sunday to learn that the Carfort relatives had called with all the family news. Jock, who was still fighting to keep on his feet, and who looked on himself as a useless man in moments of deep depression, had invited them to his place, both from Carfort and Glenmark. Jock's farmhand had just married locally, and that meant that they did not need to fear that he might leave them in the busiest time of the year. Jock treated the man as a brother, and sometimes Fay was glad to depend on his wife to relieve herself on trips to town for Jock's tablets.

Peter also spoke of a National Loan that was going to be launched for which he planned to have a joint subscription with her and added with a schoolboy's delight that he had sold a trailerload of turf as he had a surplus. And Jay told her of Luxo's escape from a lorry the day before. When the men were absent a little later in the evening, Terna re-read her old pal's letter, only to find that she had not read it fully, rushing away. The writer had expressed regret over Vane's indisposition. How news travels! the friend had heard it in New York only a week before and it must certainly have been tearing at her heart-strings. She had even mentioned the name of a doctor in New York who might cure him. Terna answered the letter at once. The character of the first woman showed in her actions as well as her words. Looking across the gulf of years and remembering, calls for a depth of feeling. Her son returned with a message, and she had still another confrontation with him as to what he meant to be before he reached manhood. His answer was neither naive nor vague.

'I'm sick of myself, Mammy! And I'm *sick* looking at *you* trying to keep smiling between all the pressures. And you do not laugh as much now as you used to do.' She made tea.

'Can't you help me to laugh as I used to, Jay!'

'I – I – can't, I can't. I – I – should do, but – I – I can't.' His eyes were sad. 'It's something inside in me, something in myself that keeps me back, keeps me here running messages like a child and kicking a ball for exercise when I feel like it. And it's an age of automation.'

Terna went to him sympathetically. 'Jay! don't see it that way. You will only hurt yourself. These are only in-between days in your life. I can see it. Keep your faith shining! Time is for using and life is much of a mental struggle for everybody.'

Jay forgot about hanging about for the moment, for he rose and pegged a basketful of clothes on the line in the garden, a stiff wind winding the sheets around him. Peter came in. Peter rarely discussed Jay's future with him at all since his first outburst. And from then on the mother started to make sacrifices for Vane's cure and for Jay's ultimate decision. Peter rose from the table, warmed himself at the big grate full of live coals, and soon went out on patrol after attaching his baton to his belt. Jay then did the wash-up before he retired to his room.

The next post was interesting, for Gay had written a long description of the man she intended to marry and to whom she had just become engaged. George Honan was his name and he was an optician by profession. Gay said that she had written to Blitz already, to Blitz who promptly expressed her surprise that her sister should even entertain such a thought for a few more years. Gay invited her nearest relatives to England to meet her fiancé and his people but they could not get away just then, for Peter had it in mind to accept the invitation of their German friends as soon as possible and conveyed this to Gay by the next post, and again when they rang her on her birthday, when he spoke to his future son-in-law for the first time.

Yes, this was different, different from the contents of those hateful, brown envelopes that were dropped into the letter box frequently, and the words: 'Vane is unchanged.' Though at that period when Terna began to go without, she experienced another kind of uplift, doing something for somebody new; a reaching to a maturity that would be spiritually enriching. She had given up what she considered vitally necessary before, the daily consumption of T-bone and porter-house steak for lunch, and substituted a vegetable diet with fish and rice and eggs from the country. Peter warned her that reducing the intake of iron in her food could lead to anaemia. Blitz seconded this and spoke of the danger of cholesterol diet.

Blitz also told them that she had got a few firsts in a Law examination, and Peter mentioned an unfair demand for Income Tax that he had received in her absence. Terna directed him to have a thorough investigation into the case, and predicted a refund which he received in due course. Terna was beginning to be just a bit out of her depth, and once she slipped away on her own to pour out her feelings in a composition about Vane. It began:

> O, my son, beacon of all the years,
> The sunlight when you knew life,
> And now missed and mourned,
> filling us with greater pride
> than ever before, for you
> suffer in silence and goodness,

*nobler in ailing manhood*
*than in unthinking youth*
*before the cruel swipe smote*
*you into dull vacuity,*
*And you knew the pain*
*That evermore companions you;*
*While a mother's mood, expectant,*
*prays you away from the rawness*
*of your life. But that other thing,*
*death in life, is still your lot.*
*God! give me my son!*
*With seven gifts endowed,*
*void in him now since he knows*
*no blessing of health.*
*Power! give back my son,*
*bright as your promises and*
*your prayer rewards, a Victor.*

Having written that, she had said all she ever wanted to say for the rest of her life. It relieved her and saddened her together until she folded it and locked it away with her other literary build-ups. The time for Peter's German visit was drawing near and she left nothing undone to help him enjoy it. He had been showing signs of fatigue just then. Before he left he pointed out to Jay about the real necessity of reading good books at all times, how one could correct and perfect oneself and escape from empty monotony. 'See Blitz, the polyglot, the purist who hates slang! What she has done, you can do. You might even scrap your worthless decisions.' Jay was moved at his father's concern for him all the way. The youth felt mean and self-reproachful after that and waited hand and foot on his mother.

Not to be forgotten was the interest Terna took in lotteries, sweeps and especially the Conquer Cancer Campaign. She won in it and followed it up, not so much for wins but for the good it might do to sufferers from that dreadful scourge. She even got Jay interested in it.

Peter had rung from Dublin before he had got on the plane, so her mind was easy, and though she had been seized with a longing to see Jock, she had the same wish to tackle the garden which had not been so well looked after since Madge's and her own joint effort.

She wrote a list including squares for the landing and bathroom, and trousers for Jay, and then sent him all the way to Galway city to purchase them. Pulling on her gloves and equipped with rake, hoe and saw, she worked until she became thirsty and hungry with a touch of headache. Backbending, straightening, and gathering grasses and weeds for the compost heap, took their toll. Some of the weeds were deep-rooted and she had to use a fork to eradicate them fully. Standing to view her progress, she discovered that it was already afternoon. She looked up at the sky and saw irregular clouds profiled against it. She worked until the shorter rays of evening sunlight made place for shadows. It had done her good to be out there, listening to the ascending scale of the breezes in the only tree in it. How activity in the open suited her! Also Peter who was really a walking enthusiast.

As she approached the back door with her tools the smell of frying rashers reached her nostrils through the inch of open window, and Jay was opening the door to admit her. She laid the tools aside before she came in. He had hurried home because she was alone, and he took a tentative step to spring a surprise on her. He would not allow her to touch the cumbersome shopping until they had partaken of the repast, though her share consisted only of eggs, the usual calories and the pears that he had brought her, for she had eaten more fruit since she had given up meat. They enjoyed the meal with radio music and discussed the details of the day. The mother stole a look at her son's brilliant face, his sweep of forehead, and wondered, wondered. Even though she finished first, she waited patiently for Jay's hands to open knots and cut chords on the parcel and to show her the things she ordered. Nothing could be more pleasing than what she saw, the red carpet for the landing space near the bathroom door, and purple pieces for the bathroom the same shade as the walls and other mats. She could be compared to a teenager having her dress sense gratified.

She gripped Jay by the shoulders playfully and then mounted the stairs with the pieces to lay them down. When he was putting away delph after washing up, she returned and slipped the change that he had left on the window into his pocket, gratefully. Then they rounded off the evening by visiting the husband of the dead friend who had been advised by her doctor not to marry. The second wife was an astute and pleasant woman. They had one child who took after her father in every respect.

The son of the first marriage had emigrated to England after five years in college. Terna had considered him a good makings, and like

Jay he did not like dancing. The gardening had refreshed the mother so much that she was not tired the day after. She slipped out to early Mass as usual, and as she walked along the quiet, little streets of Glenmark she chatted with a few of its residents. One of those commented on the fact of her regular church-going and 'that she might go straight up when she would draw her last.' Another woman was of the opinion 'that grace would carry anyone on the right road,' while a third, a fairly old man who was a little deaf, roared with blinking eyes that 'good people have more trouble than bad ones, and 'twas a fine thing to have patience.' Listening to him them, Terna added the pieces together and called it a sermonette that was worth retaining and repeating to Jay and the rest of the family. On account of delaying, the postman overtook her and handed her the mail.

# CHAPTER 25

# Vacations and After

As the weather changed, Terna had to defer her garden pleasures. She sat down to read the letters from Peter, Gay and Blitz. Peter's were short and there were two of them, as he posted them within a few hours of each other. He was having a wonderful time with Herr Hans Endriss and his young wife Johanna at a place called Leinfelden, eight miles from Stuttgart. Stuttgart was surrounded by sloping hills where grapes grew, and Leinfelden had flat scenery. He visited Baden Baden, the Black Forest and Frankfurt on Maine. Germany was a highly industrialized country with hospitable people, easy to talk to and most understanding about his language difficulties. His friends could converse in English. One hour was more enjoyable than the other and his host did not allow him to become over-tired. Peter's stay was over all too soon and he talked of Germany for months after.

Peter loved to see things through and had a knack of making things alive when described them. His hearers frequently thought that they were looking through a very clear prism while he spoke. Jay and Terna had much to occupy them and they were preparing for another visit to Vane by then.

Of course they had expected the vacant stare, the alienation, the crouching and the timidity that had gripped him, the silence instead of spontaneous communication and expressions in the Gold Medal bracket. The River Suck was a short distance from the hospital and patients like Vane were brought on short tours around there as a form of therapy. But Vane never noticed the new glimmerings of the cool morn, never heard the sweet exchange of birds or saw the silver sheen of mist rising from the river. He was flesh, blood and bone only.

Terna always had a slight flush of uneasiness the moment before her son would appear. This time she was prepared and equal to it. They packed Vane into a car and headed for a Midland town. Halfway there they stood on a grassy hill and enjoyed some goodies until Vane grew restless and they continued their journey. Oh! for one word from Vane! After saying goodbye to him they drove home quickly and went out of their way to visit a certain family. There was a friendly air there and they stayed long into the night for a music session and the son of the house obliged with a rendering of old and new songs which was a vocal treat. The night was neither dark nor bright with just enough moonlight to create an exquisite aura, a pervasiveness that was to last until the dawn showed and the face of the sun appeared.

Terna was to be engaged in professional domesticity without being fully confined to the house, for many weeks after that. Now and then, the usual snatches of inspiration came to her, like unbidden orders. For instance, when the late Pope Pius XII, whose secular name was Eugene Pacelli, was ailing, she knew that she had to write some lines about his life and death. The piece was just completed when His Holiness died, 'the spent shepherd departed from the lonely lea,' as she herself had said, for she had known.

Blitz could not be expected to be a superhuman factotum but she had been hatching a plan for ages, that when she would have time to play with, her mother and herself would have a European tour. Terna gave the proposal much thought before she agreed, though she was thrilled at the chance of a tour outside Ireland again. Nothing was settled until Peter joined the family three days later. Though he had written so many times he still had much to relate and that made Terna more enthusiastic about the move. After Peter's longest holiday Terna realised how bare and empty it must be for women who lose their husbands or who live apart from them. A husband is the backbone of the family. The foreign souvenirs were unusual. Peter left the decision to themselves. Blitz was a born traveller and knew all the ins and outs, the do's and the don'ts. So a motoring tour was decided on finally and Peter and his son found themselves on their own once again, though Terna ensured that an elderly woman would be there to take over, should they need her. And Peter being a good cook, they had no worries on that score. Terna herself had taught him how to cook omelettes, poached eggs and chops, and to make soup.

When Blitz became available, and all the arrangements were

complete, they left Ireland by Rosslare in Wexford on a very breezy day with sooty clouds and rain. Sometimes the rain descended in a downpour, streaming like funnelled runlets on the windscreen, and making the driver slow down. Visibility was poor for most of the journey though the showers were often followed by brilliant brooches of sun that gave the screen an engraved appearance when it was half dry.

The Rosslare terminal was crowded that day and the name of the vessel was the *Saint Patrick*. It had a very luxurious car ferry, the largest ever to sail under the Irish flag. It was two-level and could accommodate two hundred cars, even caravans were taken on. The Irish Continental line from Rosslare to Le Havre in France offered a relaxing journey to motoring tourists who derived more pleasure from it since their time was their own. The Cannings enjoyed every turn of it from once they arrived in the warmer climate, for they had been fortunate enough to have booked berths and had no illness whatsoever. They drove to Lisieux where they had the holy honour of attending Mass at the world-famous shrine of a young girl who had become a Saint in the brief span of nine years. While there Blitz decided that she would call her new house: *Bláithín,** or *Little Flower*. It was moving to see all the preserved, personal belongings of the late Saint. Terna thought of her life of sacrifices for souls and her perpetual state of grace in order to please her Creator on Whom she modelled herself.

Terna began months after:

*All who would serve the Lord with joy,*
*Go, seek Him through Thérèse.*
*She made herself His little toy*
*To break or mend or tease,*
*And so on earth did Heaven enjoy*
*For Jesus played her into dreams,*
*And He was just her little boy,*
*Her Host at morn, her Guest at ev'n.*

While abroad they toured France, Switzerland and some of Italy. The distance from Le Havre to Lourdes is 560 miles, and from Lisieux to Lourdes, 600 miles. From Lisieux they went to Alençon, the Loire Valley, Angiers, Le Mans, Saumer, Poitiers, Bordeaux, Lourdes,

---

* Pronounced *Blawheen*.

125

Toulouse, Nîmes, Avignon, Valence, La Toussuire, Cluny, Geneva, Grenoble, Lausanne, Taizè, Dijon, Accolay, Sens, Chartres, where the eighth-century cathedral looks like a heavenly gem from the surrounding heights, and lastly Fontainebleau.

There were no language difficulties for Blitz for she was fluent already. Terna had practised her French since her early days, and she, also, found that she could follow the foreigners, especially the French, by their expressions and their gestures – Blitz was highly amused at this.

They took the Lourdes waters that revived soul and body. Terna had holy envy of the girl, Bernadette, who had been privileged by seeing the apparition of the Virgin Mary as she gathered firewood many years before. And looking around at the suffering faces, she saw Vane's and prayed for him with perfect trust.

Blitz was in top form and her Karman Ghia performed beautifully on all the autobahns, the main motorways. They spent less time in Italy than they had intended to. They found the Swiss open-minded and industrious. Terna remarked that they worked with all the precision of their Geneva watches. Day followed day happily in the city and country and once they parked near wide fields of grapes in France while the midday sun poured down with matchless brilliance. Terna opened the windows fully to admit its direct beams. Blitz had tanned quickly, but Terna's skin reddened, before it darkened. On leaving the car to walk, they had many waves from other motorists who like themselves valued a look of friendship far away from their own shores. A party drew up and spoke in English though they were Spaniards. No doubt they were highly entertaining. One of them owned a chain of restaurants in his own country, and he showed them pictures of them, not forgetting to extend an invitation to the tourists from Ireland as he lifted his collapsible table from the boot and led them to help themselves to tins of salmon and fruit. The man, who talked like a poet, praised the beauty of the Irish countryside and 'its slumbering mountains keeping their ancient stand against the elements.' The foreign lady knew of Ireland's switch to modernity and industrialization.

The party exchanged the change of views, and one of them who also spoke French, remarked: 'très jolie! très jolie!' as he turned to Blitz, and she mentioned her love of poets and poetry to him. 'Bien!' he smiled, 'poets, mostly spiritual craftsmen … helping humanity …

sensitive ... *mais, mais être en minorité, maintenant, oui, oui'* ... Then he exclaimed with a flourish of delight: '*La Belle France! Bienvenues!*'

Terna accepted the cheese they offered, coming as it did from an agricultural country. At last they parted and Terna and her daughter drove slowly along the roads of the south when a huge vehicle drove round a bend at a high speed and missed an impact by less than a fraction of an inch. The driver of the other vehicle never stopped when there was not an actual collision. That was before they had ordered *deux petite tranches de porc.* Blitz consulted her map in the third week of their tour with a view to returning to England and to visit Gay. The French officials were kind.

On arrival in England they were ready for a sight-seeing bout of London, but this had to wait. Instead, they picked suitable gifts for different people.

Gay's place was twelve miles from London. Her house was situated between green fields, and was only a few minutes' walk from a shopping centre. Young trees, evenly spaced, grew along the grassy margin of a sidewalk there. Everything was in order in her place and the visitors' room was at the back, facing the garden. This meant that a sleeper was not bothered by passing cars at night. There was an air of peace there that Terna valued after weeks on wheels and broken sleep; the babble of foreign tongues and dialects of diverse types of humanity. It was good to see Gay in exuberant spirits. Her husband George was absent when they called but returned from work a few hours later. They invited them to stay. What a blissful week!

Gay arranged a guided tour of London for her mother and herself two days later while Blitz visited friends in Park Lane who attended London University. Gay thought that the guide's directions were slipshod.

Terna and her elder daughter slipped into London, visiting Harrod's emporium with its rich variety of merchandise, Fortnam and Mason, Selfridges, Swan and Edgar, and Bentalls of Kingston-on-Thames where they purchased pink and blue coats, and where Gay fancied a brown leather coat, though her mother advised her not to wear anything so dull with her fair colouring.

When they came back, Terna suggested a run to Ealing, so Blitz joined them and while there she had her eyes tested. There is a Common in Ealing. They browsed in bookshops, old and new. How that second daughter poured over volumes, always, often switching off the light in the bedroom when 'Aurora parted the shades with trembling hands and slim,' to quote a line of her mother's poem on the dawn. (1940?) Terna often questioned the wisdom of her constant and prolonged study outside her required application. As for the run from Ealing, Gay and all soon squeezed into their seats in the car between the piles of books, new editions which Blitz had fixed in there.

Gay's in-laws owned a houseboat, the *Vernette*, which was moored on the Thames. The river is the same size as the Shannon that rises in the Cavan mountains. A few times during their stay, when the quiet waters were as smooth as silk, the owner of the boat had the pleasure of relaxing in it and watching the changing clouds above or their reflection at noon on the river's glassy surface. The boat was sixty feet long with all the necessary amenities and a comfortable interior. Another interesting feature of their stay in the London suburb was the performance of the play *No, No, Nanette* at the Theatre Royal in Drury Lane with Anna Neagle starring. The design on the programme was copied from the original Chapter of King Charles II in 1663. All this time Terna was mentally hoarding impressions, notes and descriptive phrases, just as she had done on her solo cycling tours to date and on her excursions to wild and wide country places, or Kilcross, Loughrea and Gort in South Galway in retrospect. Those airy expanses never failed to exercise a near mesmeric play, almost a cloying pressure, when the merest points of punctuation in many alternatives were screened before her mental vision.

So when the four hundred and fifty miles between their English address and Cane Street had to be covered, Gay persuaded her mother to remain over for a day so they could both fly to Ireland, and she could spend a short holiday with her family. Just what her mother wished to hear for she loved to see the children come, as it made up for Vane's absence to a certain extent. Blitz accepted invitations from her friends in Weybridge, the Vintners, and from Miss Elizabeth Moberly, granddaughter of the Moberley family. The young lady was studying Theology in Oxford University.

# CHAPTER 26

# *Home Interests*

Terna and Gay left Heathrow Airport at 10.50 a.m. and arrived in
Dublin less than an hour after. The pilot had shown some nervousness
at first as there was a slight fog, but Terna was quite optimistic that
it would clear up and so it did ... Gay's days in Ireland were good
ones, for both her parents and Jay left nothing undone to entertain
and amuse his 'sweet lady'. Peter was delighted with the change in
Terna. She had lost the look of maternal anxiety; *Die Mutter hat
Angst*, as Vane had once said it. Gay had grown thinner and had
developed. She had a successful marriage like her parents.

Jay and Gay enjoyed games of Scrabble, table tennis, golf and
walking in the long, narrow roads around home. Then, for the last
two days of her stay her father had planned a mystery tour. It was
an area of the West where there were stretches of stony ground with
scant vegetation, and grazed by undersized, horny, sheep. When they
returned there were old friends of Gay's, now all married, there to
meet her, after they had finished their jobs in town; one of those
informed her that the doctors had just given up Giraffy, the man of
many moods and much property. And for Gay, it was goodbye to
Glenmark after an unsuccessful attempt to entice Jay to accompany
her. No doubt, Jay was deeply attached to where his roots were, yet
Terna believed that time would deal wisely with the situation, for she
was a woman of faith. For months after, Terna's literary inclinations
lay in composition of a religious kind. And once again, long country
walks stood to her for she had become subject to headaches. Peter
was pleased she never missed a day in the open. Those walks meant
a veritable feast for her, for she used to watch the change in the skies,

the colours and the fall of acorns in the great, overlapping branches of the oaks by the roadsides and in the way leading to the heath, where crab-apples grew unattended. The wild fruits looked all the better for having the dust washed off them by the showers. Like the other hedge food, the berries, they need no cultivation. And their natural bitterness can become a gastronomic delight with some sweetening. Crab-apple and blackberry jam were her husband's favourites and he always looked forward to their season.

On one such evening as Terna entered the house, there was a television announcement about her Abbeyleix lyric which had appeared already in a newspaper. Later on, when the same piece appeared in a Galway paper, Blitz happened to have a poem on The Rising, 1916, in Irish, in the same paper. Terna spent many happy moments putting an air to *Abbeyleix*, though never fully satisfied with any of the attempts. Peter had a good ear, so he often acted as critic and adviser. He thought that the song called for slower airs than any of hers. Once, on her regular intakes of ozone and oxygen, she raced into the house and said brightly: 'Little hills and mountainy places are so inspiring, Peter! I know.'

'I am afraid I do not find boglands inspirational, Terna! That is only theory. I see turf in them, that is all.' He switched off the set. 'But I mean – I mean the sight of such places and what they convey to me, afford some relief, a weaning from the horrid thought of Vane's illness.' She ceased and began again like one to whom another dictated.

'Life is freedom when acceptance and gratitude go together; it is slavery when uplifting theories are cast aside for hard-core beliefs that leave no room for aesthetic attractions and enlightenments. In hopeful moments I see Vane sitting amongst us with his educated wit and a shining face.' She thought hard. 'His darkness will be buried ocean-deep yet.'

Peter smiled. 'You are geared for optimism,' laying his hand on her shoulder, 'it is flowing over.'

'I cannot help it, and I need it, though I cannot make things happen.'

As she prepared chops he fell silent, and taking the meal after, he began: 'You are making me think of Vane's word about poetry and inspiration.'

'Oh! what did Vane say, Peter? Tell me. I know it will have an impact afterwards.'

'Well, Vane loved the verbal music of some poetry, and he liked clear depths when the mind and imagination worked at it. He loved rich sounds.'

'As much as he loved right, Peter! What a pity his life and prospects have been ruined! Vane!!'

'Vane, just that!' he sympathised. He switched on again and they both concentrated on the programme until it was time to retire. And Terna knew that both wakening and sleeping would be filled with little floating images looking like Vane, Gay, Blitz and Jay at different ages.

A week or so after that satisfying discussion Terna dragged downstairs to see the postman approach struggling with parcels, letters and a publication on the inception of the Garda Siochana in 1922, which Peter had ordered from Easons of Dublin. Heavier than that, however, was a full set of Staffordshire pottery from Gay, with a design of Autumn leaves and tints on the cups, and the name of 'Gay Fantasy'. While Peter perused his books Terna saw a massive box of chocolates addressed to herself, and she hardly breathed until she readdressed it to Vane. When she returned some minutes after, she saw Peter in the new suit that he had ordered in a Dublin store some weeks before; he had to wear outfits made to order which he fitted a few times. His wife admired it as she began to unpack the precious twenty-one pieces with the intention of removing them to the dining room later. A kind of joy was welling up in her so she returned to the letters, looking over them briefly until she opened the last one and gasped. The news it contained shocked and saddened her; she had lost fifteen hundred pounds, plus six months' interest on it through the company getting into difficulties. She was speechless for hours and the rest of that week was like a long, dark night with the already ruffled stream of their lives rising to a swollen, angry sea, beating and lashing them like pale pebbles on its cold shore. Peter was very sympathetic as she said:

'Such an entry for the family diary! Happiness seems so far away, and too much of the opposite makes a stone of the kindest heart.' She sat on the sofa.

'Really, we should begin to keep a diary of our sorrows.'

'Not that, anyway, Terna! We cannot tell ourselves that this has not happened, I know, but we will keep looking forward.'

'Yes, I suppose, there must be a way of redeeming the situation, so much in the pound might be forthcoming.' She picked up a letter from Blitz to read.

'We do not know yet,' he told her. 'Wait.'

Then she mentioned Blitz's decision to become a nomad with widening, literary interests.

'A nomad.'

'Just that. She begins a world tour soon, as soon as time permits,' she said, putting down the letter.

'Oh! In the next long vacation. Well, she is wise and capable of minding herself on foreign highways. And she makes friends easily wherever she goes, whereas Gay is cautiously hesitant before she becomes familiar with others. Different types. No two are really alike even in the same family.' Then he rose and pulled on his uniform jacket about to leave. 'You have mentioned acceptance, so we must accept our young people are growing older and neither of us will ever see fifty again.' He climbed the stairs with surprising agility for his fifty-odd years. And as he moved off a minute later, she noticed that the patches of grey at his temples were increasing while her own hair was only thinning a little. And then the front door was closed. Despite the new pressures and the raw uncertainty, a happy moment presented itself when she mentally approached the frontiers between prose and poetry, and she began jotting and dotting a page to be filled in as the fighting in Belfast flashed before her mind. The work was to be titled 'Child of Peace,' and sent to a provincial paper ultimately for Christmas inclusion, the second most important Feast of the year in her eyes.

The discipline that was called for while she worked on it was very rewarding. Alternatives came to mind easily every time ... Household jobs kept her occupied in the late evening and then it was time for Peter's return from duty, and she heard 'Terna' at the window before he stepped in. She laid aside the spotless tea-cloth that she had just handled.

'Yes, Peter!'

'I was thinking things over on duty.'

'Thinking, there are so many things.'

'It is that whatever about ozone and oxygen, on mountain passages, your headaches never fail to come back.'

'I am used to them,' she smiled, 'do not worry, they are the least of my troubles.'

'I realise that, but what I've been thinking about is that you could do with another run to your favourite beauty spots in Ireland.'

She almost cut him off and grew very serious.

'Impossible. Any more solo tours are out for me, I am afraid. I am just not anxious.

He considered. 'There is no rush. What about our single daughter spending some time here before she departs to the other side of the world?'

She thought for a moment as she prepared coffee. 'I do not know, Peter! The decision must rest with Blitz.' And while she spoke a wire that her brother Jay had died suddenly in Cratton, arrived. Hasty preparations followed the initial regret even as they continued speaking ... She passed the coffee to Peter first. When he had left she began to iron the clothes, and one job followed another until she felt like relaxing, mentally and physically. From where she sat in pleasant composure she could see the light fading outside, but the steely blue of the sky was visible still. Little winds whimpered at the partly-open window and grew silent again, when the mingled dozy whispers of retiring birds in the hedge near the laburnum tree could be heard faintly. And catching the lulling sounds, Terna herself dozed off into a careless oblivion ...

The grating of a key outside roused her to full consciousness and Peter came to her side at once. She knew by the set of his profile that he had contacted Blitz, and to good effect; that he also had the pleasure of hearing her speak. Blitz was to be in the house within a certain time and there was to be a motoring tour of the North-West from different directions. For a spell, the habit of making ideas crystallise into images was to be left severely alone, for a wonder. After the funeral the next day Terna was on the way to the optician for an eye test, though she hated the idea of wearing spectacles. The three of them were engaged from morning to night, Peter more on his official work, as it happened, and the others on their own. Terna herself missed a good while on the local boglands in order to square things for the coming event. At the end of a few weeks she would set about replenishing the fridge, baking bouts and bouts of cakes and confectionery, ordering a joint and groceries that would be at hand for her husband and son. She wished them to have a holiday at home with Jay indulging his love for soccer, with golf and table tennis as pleasant extras.

As for Peter, he would browse at the books all over the heated house as well as his large collection of Digests, play records, and entertain unexpected friends, both in uniform and plain clothes. Jay would not read as he had a decided distaste for it by then. It was hard to remain optimistic in the face of that. And neither of the two would kill an evening over a few rounds in a pub, for they both had a natural disgust for it. As far as Peter was concerned he had never considered drink as an antidote to anything. The fact that he had sometimes witnessed rowdy scenes in town and country quickened his susceptibilities as to what happened when the intoxicated brain became fuddled, with the victim no longer capable of coherent expression, much less normal procedure.

As a follow-up, it is not just out of pride in their sobriety or contempt of those who over-indulged in alcohol, that the following incident is included, concerning a married woman. A man began to make a positive nuisance of himself with his passionate declarations to her. *How she recoiled from those unwelcome attentions*! The unfortunate addict rambled more and more about his attachment until he became purely contemptible. That drunkard's attachment ruined a friendship that started with neighbourly reminiscences. Sadly enough, it terminated in the sick man, the alcoholic, tumbling head over heels into an excavation pit where pipes were being laid for a water supply. People marvelled at the comfortable and composed appearance of the staggerer in the hole where he remained until he sobered up. Had the weakling thought of marriage as a yoke of preservation for the contracting parties, even a spiritual insurance for them and a state to be respected, there should never have been any such thing as an amorous approach. An approach that could have been full of consequences, had not the dictates of charity spared the addict and sent him on his way. Marriage is an inviolable institution but it is not impregnable ...

# CHAPTER 27

# *Short Travels*

The landing was another ideal spot to stand and think for it faced the open. Terna would place an elbow on the sash and try to recapture the mood of her richer meditating, taking all together, day, night, bogs, skies, rain, snow, fields, dawns, flowers, stars, streams, views, mostly of the country where she enjoyed so many distant, and, therefore subdued, sounds that were never distracting.

The fields that stretched away at the back of Cannings now looked dim and uninviting and the spaces above them were a cold grey like wintry dawn light. Still the magic of it all held her and she did not wish for any aesthetic effects or inspirations, only to let the sight sink in as she closed her eyes, fully receptive. Then she opened her eyes and began to summarise the things that made her a whole and happy person. And just then all the lights in the house went off and she had to grope around until she found a knob of a bedroom door. Peter's bicycle lamp might be lying about, maybe his matches at hand so she could hunt for a candle; or Peter's saving presence itself any minute at all to remedy the matter. She waited. Then she gave thanks for the power of thought as she felt her way to the top of the stairs and found the bannister, just as a jetty cloud rolled in the lower sky and left a lighter patch which showed through the window and relieved the darkness on her way down to the hall.

She then entered the living room and passed out to the scullery to feel around for the candle stumps, so that by the time her husband turned up, there was a vague, an uncertain, flickering brightness to cheer him. 'There has been a power cut,' he explained, glad of the way Terna had come to the rescue. He had bought her favourite magazines and the evening papers. And as the light was faulty, she prepared a salad for him which he relished.

The remote preparations for their run were well under way. The weather had changed. It made a soft, misty air and the people of Glenmark availed themselves of it. Most conspicuous were the twos and threes who appeared in earnest conversation on the roads, the five main roads leading from the town. It looked as if the strollers had been freed from the tiresome restrictions of too much modernity, and amenities that called for care and attention in another way. Businessmen found the runs most stimulating and they adapted the happy habit of driving so far with their wives and children and taking constitutionals among the hills that rose here and there before they faced the town again. It is wonderful how people are influenced by others. Turns in the open had become so popular then, that a certain family locked their premises every day to get away for a time. It went on for weeks.

And into this changed condition came the hooting of the horn of the Karman Ghia and Blitz at the wheel. Blitz's glowing spirits were spilling over on everybody in a short time. Her yellow outfit was the same shade as the car. She promptly told her parents of the extreme kindness of the people who gave her an extra day off on account of the long journey home. The family retired late that night and by the afternoon of the next day, after the car had a wash and polish, the mother and daughter began an interesting tour in warm clothes. They saw the small North Galway town where the Augustinian Abbey had been closed by Protestant reformers in 1539, when the priests took up residence in a house in Louthlodge, in the townland of Lissybroder. A very valuable Chalice that was in use there was later used by the members of the same order in Ballyhaunis. The former Abbey had been used for Protestant services for some years until their scant numbers died out.

Leaving the ruin of the Abbey, they passed through the countryside of Curraghwest to the town of Castlerea where they lunched and viewed television later. The town was prosperous and resembled Ballyhaunis. Their next stop was the village of Loughglynn where a very kindly poultry instructress introduced herself and they conversed until 3.15 p.m. A mile or so from there the weather and their spirits changed. Thunder and lightning spoiled the evening and Terna had the presence of mind to remove her spectacles that she had grown used to already. They drove faster until they reached Ballaghadereen in the County Roscommon. The town was much like Glenmark in north County Galway. Terna gleaned a few interesting things about it from an old resident. In days gone by, rather in the distant past, forty-eight families from Syria who had to leave their own country through over-population, had settled in Ballaghadereen where they set to work with their hands to build underground passages, leading to the four altars of Edmundstown. The four altars had been erected in the open so priests could offer the sacrifice of the Mass in penal times when monasteries were confiscated and their lands divided on others.

They observed the milestones along the old coach roads long before the trains and buses came. The first railway line was opened in England between Stockton and Darlington in 1835, and between Dublin and Dun Laoghaire a few years later. Then after more refreshments they rested for a while, and were agreeably surprised later when the air had cleared near Gurteen, a village in the County Sligo, thirty-six miles from home. From there they turned to Ballymote, seven miles distant, and struck up an aquaintance with another lady who lived in Rathmullen, passed a creamery on the way and arrived at a place in Donegal where they overnighted.

The next day, the feast of Corpus Christi and also of Saint Antony, they attended Mass at 10 a.m., breakfasted and decided to return to Sligo town where they called on a friend, a Miss Tansey, and later attended a Court proceedings: a case of hire purchase, a question of handwriting, and the case was dismissed. Terna was delighted, for judging from outward appearances, the defendant was in very poor circumstances. Blitz followed every detail as she had already mentioned a Law Degree. When the Court was over, Terna and her daughter enjoyed a most delicious lunch in the Grand Hotel in Sligo. They paid a visit to the Museum and Library where Terna had a small edition of verse on loan. It was a short visit and they set out for Glencar of the beautiful waterfall, lake and mountains; of many deserted cottages and where Blitz suggested a round of the Rosary, at a wayside shrine, the Roman Catholics' practice of saluting The Mother of God in her Son's mysteries.

They had to skip over rough stones to reach the shrine, some stones solid enough and others so loose that the travellers found it difficult to get a hold. They spent hours in Glencar, that holiday haunt of the currents supposed to be so dangerous for bathers.

The next place in their itinerary was Drumcliffe where the poet William Butler Yeats was buried and where his father was Rector. As they walked in the cemetery with some few people, Terna explained what the poet had meant by: 'Cast a cold eye on life,' the words on his headstone. She punctuated the passage mentally. An introduction to a Headmaster of a college followed with an interesting discussion on schools, education and the problem of getting brilliant children who dislike study to like it. They headed for another village then, which was surrounded by unusually green pasture. It was Grange. They remained for an hour when Blitz wrote some letters in the car and Terna fell into a happy silence. So they moved to the more rugged splendors of Donegal, passing Lissadel and Classiebawn.

The third day of their run saw them in Bundoran, the stronghold of Gilmartins. There Terna purchased a newspaper, the *Donegal Democrat*, also the *Derry Journal*. Other buys were blouses and skirts on the strand, and after that they sent a pile of letters and cards describing places and people to Glenmark, Carfort, Dublin, Longford, Cratton, London and Kilcross.

They had an early lunch that day for they wished to go to Bally-shannon where the Poet Allingham was born in 1829. There they ordered souvenirs in Stephens' modern store and passed through Balinatra, Laghy and Lady Hamilton's residence, right into Donegal town to view O'Donnell's castle, to visit furniture stores and to buy fruit; also a visit to McGee's and Timmoney's. Enniskillen and Fermanagh beckoned then, and getting there proved to be a linguistic treat, for they met a German tourist and industrialist who conversed in his own language with Blitz all the way. Blitz was so fluent that the man refused to believe that she was not of German descent, even a countrywoman of his. All three of them drove to see the Monument to the Four Masters. When they parted the Cannings enjoyed the Methodist Conference on television by Reverend T. Lindsay. They slept well in a very comfortable place called 'Glena' while in Bundoran. A meal elsewhere was horrible, a messy bacon lunch where Terna had expected a better culinary effort from the owner, who had, really, a good reputation. Owing to their short stay, Terna tactfully decided not to show her disappointment.

After the indifferent meal the travellers set out for Kinlough, in the direction of Leitrim. Again they bought papers, the *Irish Times* and the *Impartial Reporter*. At a place called Largydonnell, they left the car and walked slowly into the country, Terna to lose a touch of a headache and Blitz to read Russian poetry. Half an hour passed, away from the main traffic, for they were on green ground with a low line of young trees and a background of hillocks that would be greener later on. It was a place to charm artists, photographers and naturalists, especially when sun glints played in the trees and the Leitrim breezes danced in them. But such delights were not given to last. As a few hidden throats began their silky notes in a hedge, the relentless rain fell and the strollers had to seek cover or be drenched. They looked at the sky, the dripping trees, and thought that the mountains were nearer than they had been at first. How to get back then before Blitz's precious volume would be ruined from cover to cover, and her hair in little twists that looked like water-rats' tails? And her mother calm and possessed with odd drops escaping down her neck while she planned an initiative? Strangers soaking in a strange place! And two rain-proof garments hanging in the car! The unceasing rain continued until all of a sudden it did not matter, for a few English people in an Austin car drew up, understanding the difficulty, and conveyed them instantly to their own car in a matter of minutes. Such a relief!

Blitz placed her damaged book near the windscreen so that the sun might dry it, if it shone, and she also turned on the heat. For the rest, they could not change until they reached Manor Hamilton where they changed and where Terna bought a roomy house-coat and beautiful, feminine articles for Blitz that would serve as accessories for her different suits.

They were both enchanted at the small dwellings in from the road, here, too, they were so colourful. Then Blitz discovered that she had lost or mislaid her dark glasses, and they drove back to Bundoran just in time for tea. The Polaroid glasses were never found. Fairly sad, they went to the television room for the news and a good programme: 'Farewell to the Old Vic', and bed after, Terna wondering how Sir Laurence Olivier had preserved his stage presence all through his acting career, being somebody else all the time.

The two women rose at nine o'clock next morning to breakfast early and to have Mass in time. Looking around, Blitz remarked that the Saint Louis nuns were all over the place. Then towards midday, when the sun shone as brightly as new diamonds, they began another tramp out, as a compensation for one spoilt one. They passed by the

Great Southern Hotel, on by the Atlantic to Tullagh Strand, where a certain native called Black made a very good impression on them as they chatted.

It must be said that they found the place more bracing than any inland part of County Galway. And to grow all the more invigorated, they walked briskly until they reached the car again. As it was Sunday there were crowds in Bundoran, so Terna asked Blitz to see some of lower Bundoran before they started for Rosknowlagh, then to Bally-shannon, and to the left for the new Franciscan Settlement, and being directed further by an Agricultural Adviser who was travelling that way. Blitz thought that he looked like her Uncle Jock. And as it was Sunday they attended the Rosary and made the Stations of the Cross in the evening. Then it was more television, until close-down, soft drinks, bath and bed.

They went to Enniskillen again the following morning via Bally-shannon and Beleek. Here they visited the Bloomfield china factory that was established in 1857. The factory employed one hundred and twenty workers. They saw the River Erne as they drove on to County Cavan. The river rises in Lough Gowna in Cavan. The old name of the place was Scrabby where Peter's landlord ancestors lived. A wealthy family, Doppings, had an estate there. The Erne is about the same size as the Suck and the Inny. Where they parked they were approached by a foreign couple for tourist information, who had brought their two Siamese cats with them on holiday.

The healthy distractions of those days stood out in Terna's memory. Blitz considered it as a geographical interest. She shopped for glasses before they left for Swanlinbar and from there to Ballinamore, Fenagh and quiet Kesh Carrigan where they ordered snacks and tea. Back in Leitrim and feeling very refreshed they made no delay until they reached the town of Mohill where they had a discussion on Volkswagen cars with a very well-informed garage owner while he carried out a routine check on the Karman Ghia. From there they faced Carrick-on-Shannon where a genial bank clerk recommended the 'Villa Rosa' to stay in. And being tired out, they retired early and slept until 10 a.m. They particularly disliked the fact that there were twelve people staying there who must not have gone to bed at all. At breakfast they spoke to English people about soccer and learned that players were paid a hundred pounds per week there. Then it was books and more books for Blitz until her mother teased her about being a 'bookaholic' while she herself bought *Life and the Theatre*. Both laughed, and on account of Blitz's love of Irish she changed the new word to 'Leabhairaholic',* without calling herself a coiner.

---

\* *Leabhair* is Irish for books and is pronounced llower.

# CHAPTER 28

# *Returning*

At this point Terna was rather exhausted, and the fumes of petrol sickened her, so after several drinks of soda water, they left for Boyle to see the Abbey that was founded in 1161. They had a meal in The Royal after which they stocked up in a supermarket, and then drove out past the Railway bridge to Frenchpark round the Curtin, Stafford King-Harman estates. The latter mansion had been burnt by accident before then. A turn in a wood proved relaxing then. It was like entering another world. The ancient trees were like solid sentries on guard. The silence seemed to deepen and Terna paused for a teeming moment that nobody but herself could understand, and of which nobody could deprive her. Wheels were wheels, money was made to spend, save and exchange; it kept people alive physically and gave them a sense of belonging to the world even while the world of man earned their souls' worth. The tops of the massive trees met, but lower down there was room for the sylvan siblings to catch the light.

Blitz had slipped away by this time, and Terna became more wood-nymph than person. She stood, as silent as the wide wood of little paths and old leaves, and wished that she could share that priceless peace forever. The words calm, umbrage, depth, stately, age, solitude, occurred to her. Blitz came to her side then and they turned to Tulsk and Castleplunkett where a surprisingly wintry wind almost swept them off their feet while they were around the village. Then Balintubber came into view as they moved off, where there is an eight hundred-year-old ruin once owned by the Burke family of Ballyduggan, County Galway. After that it grew colder and they raced to Balleymoe and onto Glenamaddy, and full of the thoughts of home. Strange to relate, that when Terna was leaving the car in Glenmark half an hour later, she said movingly: '*We will never do this run again. Blitz!*' They had so much to tell Peter and Jay who looked suprisingly well after the few days, and so did the big house though it missed the touch of a woman's hand for that length. Jay loved the homey atmosphere again. A meat tea prepared by Terna followed and all topics of local interest were discussed at table, all but one, not a local matter by any means, and left until last to be told, better kept back yet. The day after their departure Gay's husband confirmed by letter that Gay would be undergoing a minor operation for the removal of a growth that resulted from hardening of the heel. So it could be safely assumed that the surgeon's incision had been already made and that the heel was healing. Terna admired Peter for the brave front he showed during the meal and reminded him of what he said once before in a crisis: 'We will weather the storm, Terna!' Then they waited, waited and the news arrived; Gay was fine, and glad that she had heeded her doctor. And in less than a week or so, Gay herself wrote that she was already feeling the benefit of the operation all over her. 'Only another check,' Terna said in a low voice, 'but let us be grateful that we are all alive at any rate. The chain has been broken in many families of our age group. Let us be people of faith!'

'The proper outlook, Dad, for all of us,' Blitz smiled. Terna began to write a few petitions for the Shrine of Knock where she always felt so uplifted. 'Let us go to Knock to thank and to intercede!' she urged. So the very next day they locked up and went. The four of them were like promising neophytes full of spiritual vitality when they returned three hours later, and an hour later, Peter opened the morning post to discover that Michael had died in New York.

'Michael is go-gone, Te-Terna!' And he went blindly to the Post Office and cabled the family's sympathy, when she whispered: sadly missed.

Blitz remained at home two days more for she was needed, and she looked up part I of the Law of Contract, Torts and Criminal Law. She also purchased a tape recorder and visited a dentist.

She had in her possession some old editions of tried cases which she had meant to leave behind her. The publicity given to the sins of some while other addicts managed to indulge their private devil unknown to the world of newsman! 'Welters of evil had cropped up since the world was made. People should judge with reason,' Terna

143

held. She pitied people who had not resolute wills … When her mother had finished speaking, Blitz made a list of the dates on which she would attend Dinners in the Inner Temple, London, very much later. Blitz, the bright and the good, who valued every moment of time.

When Blitz's hour of departure came the other three members of the family went with her to Dublin and saw Vane on the way up. That visit was a happy one, for his people started something that was to become a formula for him to draw him out of his dead composure. The formula consisted of taking him to the hospital canteen and telling him to call for what he wanted, then driving him into the country where he feasted on the goodies in a sheltered place with just the whisper of a breeze about. And for once, his mother asked, despairing of an answer: 'What are you drinking, Vane?' He surprised her. He mumbled, 'Lemonade, fifteen pence,' and smiled weakly. It was so like the times when he never had to think before he answered anything. She noticed his complete change of expression then, that fleeting moment.

After seeing the son whom they missed so much, safely deposited in the hospital that had been his home for almost fifteen years, they continued their journey to Dublin. The remainder of it took two hours, for the traffic was very heavy, and occasionally, drunken drivers swerved from their right side, though Blitz anticipated their action over a mile away. Having to reach the Airport at a certain time the Cannings had to content themselves with a quick, nourishing dish in a modern restaurant in Kinnegad, thirty-eight miles from Dublin. The small town of Kinnegad is like Williamstown in the north of Galway. They were soon speeding again with Jay singing at the back in a low key: 'I'll buy you a dolly', four lines and a chorus. Terna was completely lost in her song when it ended abruptly, for a tractor driven by a reckless-looking teenager dashed out from a narrow roadway leading from a house hidden in trees. And alders blocked the end of the little road where a rusty iron gate opened on to the main road. Blitz's skill prevented a collision by a hair's breadth.

Their dismay can be imagined when the offender pulled off without as much as a comment on the situation. According to Peter's knowledge of the highway code the driver with the right of way should be allowed to pass. At this juncture the country boy backed in a crooked line and knocked part of a pillar by doing so. Peter was almost explosive but Terna strongly advised against the use of abuse to become emotionally discharged. Besides the young man on the tractor was jogging away as if near collision were common to his life.

The family went to Arnott's and Jay fitted an overcoat and paid for it. Terna liked the dark grey on account of his good colouring. After a tiring day the travellers arrived home around 10 p.m. The men were as fit as ever but Terna was not. So when she had done the wash-up she stole away to work up some inspiration for 'Child of Peace'. It did her good, and to keep a literary composition moving was important to her. Already, some of the summing-up thoughts were present and alterations sprang from deep reflection and delving in her consciousness for the apt words. In fact she was so much absorbed in the work that she never heard her husband and son close the front door as they slipped out. Anyhow, quiet was necessary sometimes for her kind of work. Another title ran through her head, 'Peace Star', an alternative?

Some time after, the men returned, Peter carrying a load of briquettes and Jay helping him at the door to get through. She came to meet them and Jay informed her that the local Cinema was about to close as it did not pay to run it. More and more young people were leaving the place, especially those who had availed of the new educational opportunities offered them ...

Rather unusually for her, Terna could often be seen in the late afternoons collecting garden rubbish and old tops of plants to make manure. Sometimes she would add handfuls of lime and salt to the heap to kill any wintering pests. And knitting became interesting again as scarves, socks and gloves were always acceptable gifts for young and old. And the article she valued most was a pink, single-bed cover, designed by herself and knitted on large, wooden needles with 3-ply wool. The work had a lacy effect and some people wished to buy it. Instead, Terna gave them the easy pattern to follow, as the cover was for the visitors' room.

Gay wrote often at this stage, mentioning all details of interest. She preferred letters to the telephone. Jay and Blitz were equally good correspondents, so they were always in touch. Sometimes, though, Blitz would ring her father to trace his family tree and then enquire why her brothers were not called Philip, Charles, Robert or Bernard after the surgeons of a past generation. Peter had all the answers ready.

The next time, Blitz had a statement to make that was rather disappointing. Her second car, a Wolseley Hornet, the one she used going to lectures, had been stolen and she had already reported the theft to the police and was awaiting further developments. And another development, it happened that a prize-winning invention came to Terna just before she fell asleep one night after a busy day. It was how to knit socks with turn-down tops on two needles for children of seven and eight years, from 2½ ozs of 3-ply wool and No. 9 and 10 needles: with No. 10 needles, cast on fifty-one stitches. Knit in ribbing for about three inches, slipping at the beginning of each row to have a smooth seam behind. Change to No. 9 needles and knit plain, decreasing at each end of every sixth row until there are forty-three stitches on the needle. Then measure the sock to make sure it is long enough. Start the heel. Divide the stitches into three parts, plus two on the third *opposite* the back joining. See that the middle stitch of the heel needle is directly opposite the joining. The first row of the heel makes the *first* joining of the back seam. Put the rest of the stitches on a holder and work on the heel in the usual way until the turning is complete. Continue knitting until the sole is long enough. The toe is worked in the usual way also, but it must correspond with the overhead part of the toe. Next put the remaining stitches on a No. 9 needle, also, and knit towards the instep, decreasing at each end of every row until there are twenty-six stitches on the needle. Continue knitting until that part of the sole matches the underneath part exactly. Work the toe in the same way as before. Cast off. Press the piece well with a cool iron. Sew up the back seam as far as the ribbing. Turn the stocking inside out and sew up the ribbed part. Join the seams each side of the sole, press again and turn down ribbed parts. Darn the heels when finished to ensure long wear. It takes a few hours to knit a pair.

Creating kept Terna free from the malady of boredom. And, indeed, she had a growing concern about Jay's eyes for she had seen him close both of them so tightly again and again as he read his letters, or missal in the church. So her worst fears were confirmed a few days later when she learned from an optician that not alone had Jay very weak sight but severe conjunctivitis as well. The Cannings understood that this was inflammation of the membrane connecting the inner eyelid and the eyeball. This happened just when Peter was growing impatient at his son's open refusal to study, though his father was beginning to entertain a hope of putting him on the road to success by his doing a postal course. Through all this Gay was very philosophic. She knew the eye trouble would clear up, though there could be a recurrence of it. And Jay's eyes had always reacted to light. Maybe Jay had his own insight for so many years, since he became apathetic, from the time he had written limericks at a moment's notice and was thought to have been mildly prodigious at the age of fifteen by one of his teachers in a Secondary School. A limerick of his:

*There was an old man called Makay*
*Who worked in an oatfield all day*
*He climbed up a stack*
*And fell on his back*
*And now he is under the clay.*

written in class.

What if Jay had to suffer the affliction and the privation of total blindness, no longer capable of vision? Terna's faith sustained her again for she believed that it was faith, the thread of hope that lit up the path of her life so far. Looking at Jay, she had reason to be in a reflective mood; Jay in a deserted room for intervals during the day, and glad when the night came, to sleep off his temporary incapacity; which he did with the right remedy and attitude, a week or so before the ruthless germ of 'flu caught him and left him lying low for almost another fortnight. While his mother was nursing him the very sight of his reading, or rather stealing a squint at a soccer book without screwing up his eyes and blinking, made her happy, and especially when he did not complain of pain at the back of his eyes.

One evening as she passed from his room to the bathroom she drew aside a back curtain. A little, windy dirge like a warning note sounded in the buddleia shrub that grew beside her neighbour's boundary wall. She wondered if its lavender blooms were to be slashed, and its new growths broken, by the corner wind that blew from the back of the houses on the left. It had happened the year before, and she regretted that the shrub's soft branches were not wind-proof.

She looked at another shrub a few feet away, that had a mat of tinted leaves around its roots, wind babies that suffered all too soon, and that would become mulches in the course of time. She concluded that each shrub and tree had an individuality of its own in full beauty, but was at its best when its sap flowed upwards to form and feed leaves and buds; studded with buds, a tree became a treasure incarnate in her eyes. She went out into the first degrees of darkness and found it close and comforting, and, surprisingly, it was there that she had a moment of childhood ... she was little ... communing silently yet ably ... as the final words of 'Child of Peace' sailed into her mind:

> *In a world of erring ways and worse*
> *and no soul's home*
> *The message of the Child of Peace*
> *is Love alone.*

There were ten short verses in it. It appeared in 1966.

And so the common round of living remained when she would ask herself if Vane were to vegetate against a hospital ward for the rest of his life. And why Peter and herself were so cheerfully determined to keep faith, almost stoically so. Time was taking its toll, for what else could explain Terna's bouts of palpitations from the smallest effort when she would have to flop on the nearest seat and stop speaking. Being brave for the family's sake was truly difficult most of the time. Rest was the remedy. She had always observed the laws of health and never nibbled between meals, to avoid fatty degeneration or the other extreme, scragginess. Husband and wife always joined in the activities of their young adults on their return home without neglecting those of their own age group.

Common sense prevailed in their dealings with each other and with the children. Many entries in the Family Diary were worth a second read. Especially about Blitz visiting her uncle in America during her University course in England and Ireland, 'to drive her quietly to an Airport, that she had a lot to do.' *Had she not? Or had she?* Blitz's compensation case was going ahead, according to the latest news from Gay, and Gay herself was changing into a new house some few miles from Eton College. Peter thought that the new house cost the world and looked forward to a visit there, and like Terna, he always benefited from a change.

CHAPTER 29

# *Peter's Retirement*

Terna of Carfort could see fairly well, even far into the future, but as she enjoyed the supreme blessing of leaving good enough or bad enough alone until the next bridge had to be passed, she rarely made untimely mention of what was threatening; facing sorrows' shadows hindered one in getting to know oneself, though it is positive that a person finds his true self only when he is face to face with death.

The Cannings of Glenmark had many compensations. Their private interests flourishing and on the cultural side, their house was stocked with records from Wagner and other Masters in Russian, German, English, Irish and French, with many of Peter's favourites among them. As Terna had joined the Irish songwriters' Association earlier on, she still attended functions in Dublin once a year. There she met James Dillon-Kelly, a member of Lord Longford's company and late of the National Theatre. The actor advised her to leave Glenmark and to take up residence outside Dublin City. Success followed success for Gay and Blitz for the next few years. They had met a variety of people from the different English Universities who had similar tastes and beliefs to their own and this made for easy mixing. From the matrimonial viewpoint, nothing would induce the dynamic Blitz to marry for she was not built that way. Much later she wrote to her father to attend the George Campbell exhibition of Belfast and the troubles. The exhibitor was one of the few artists who put it all on canvas. Peter shrank from such a step as he had been reading about that deadly conflict every day already. Apart from political reasons the war was the result of deep-rooted prejudices for over three hundred years, stemming from the Plantation of Ulster, and the ultimate in brotherly bitterness ...

Terna's palpitations had eased off and her husband, son and herself used the lengthening days, the extra hours of light brought them out. And a brood of nieces and nephews once surrounded them telling them of the different scholarships they had won, and what they intended to be after five years' secondary education, and also asking an opinion on general things. When those jolly people appeared they were soon at concert pitch for the rest of the time. Terna noticed with surprise that none of them bore a close resemblance to her very handsome parents. And the faces of the new generations creased in a smile when their aunt enquired seriously if anybody prayed in the little, pink room any more!

Apart from educating their children and Blitz's graduations, the chief event of their married life was soon to come to pass. Peter was to be honourably discharged from the Force after serving for forty-four years. He retired on his sixty-third birthday in 1969, the year after the guerillas started in the North, the home of most of his ancestors. On his certificate of discharge was written the word: EXEMPLARY. And he replied suitably when given a presentation by his comrades. Many tributes were paid to him. Terna was almost beside herself with joy that the change meant an end to the official in their lives. *Civilianitis at last*, to last!

Peter took it all in his stride and had already planned a holiday in Florida and Canada, much to Terna's delight. Freedom, a rich freedom was theirs. And Peter drew a considerable gratuity on leaving. He was among the members who had opted for it by having one-fortieth of their monthly salary deducted from the day they joined.

Whenever Peter was absent the house in Cane Street was very different, less like home. Terna had certain arrears of work to be cleared up. For instance, when she was putting aside a copy of the paper containing 'Child of Peace', the end of which she had thought out in the darkness when she stood with closed eyes in its clouded softness, she began to list the other publications to which she had contributed to date: *Woman's Life*, *Woman's Way* (Ireland), the *Apostolate of The Little Flower* (America), *Ireland's Own*, the *Irish Catholic*, the *Kilkenny People*, the *Leinster Times*, the *Donegal Democrat*, the *Derry Journal*, the *Help of Christians*, the *South Galway Star*, *Tidings*, *Topic*, *Newsletters*, the *Herald* (poetry and prose), *Halcyon Days* (book form verse) and *Soulmates' Surrender* (fiction) in England.

In course of time she was very relaxed, having completed what she had set out to do, referring to pen work, of course. The following few years saw nothing noteworthy, though she dipped into adjudicating her own dramatic efforts of the past. On a day when the clear streams of sunlight made green growth paler and the new strains of young birds filled the garden, she ran upstairs just to have another look, another assessment of those literary fragments and serious creations. There they lay in one of Vane's college trunks, abandoned brain babies crushed, stained from damp, with their clips rusty and the rust around the area making the white paper a ruddy brown. Regret clutched her. Were those thousands of words lying before her to be read and forgotten some day? Why had she not approached publishers, producers, and even influential friends for their opinions and decisions? The copy where a dead spider lay was in the worst condition.

In another few years, there would not be a trace of any of them, and they would be blurred long before that. Some of them had been composed in the happy hours of her youth, some in the laden moments of middle age and then at a time when she was no longer young, even though she still had verve. She decided to spare them any further deterioration, by taking that number to the garden, setting them on fire and watching the litmus blue of the flames as they rose ... But instead, she jammed down the top of the trunk and left the room to begin a round of chores that would help her to forget her notion to destroy the work of her hands and mortify her as well.

Between general managing and runs to other towns, Terna was kept busy. Jay and herself had a very good arrangement. She never had to ask him twice to do anything. His refusal to go to College could have been purely psychological. She always respected him.

For a long time after his retirement Peter received many messages. Jay kept count of them and minded them for him. In the meantime Peter wrote every second day since he left. The heat was so oppressive out there that he had to invest in light clothes or drop down. So many vivid pictures and descriptions of Fort Lauderdale, Miami and Hollywood arrived by postcards that they had hardly anything more to learn about those places.

Peter was vastly improved and braced after the seaside where hundreds of different nationalities lay on the warm sands. A beautiful outfit of a neutral shade which he brought to Terna did not fit, and as she could not squeeze into it she earmarked it for Gay immediately. Jay liked the roomy anorak that his father gave him, and he was to wear it some time after when they both visited relatives. And at this point a wire arrived that Jock had died suddenly, so they made speedy preparations for the funeral. And that funeral was to be followed by another, for Vena's husband died suddenly, also, a week after.

During father's and son's absence later on, Terna was shopping in Glenmark on a warm day. As she approached her house she saw a tall, dark priest at the front door. He could not have been there more than a few minutes, probably had left one of the cars parked near the kerb. They spoke and she invited him in. He was a missionary who had spent seventeen years in Nigeria, and who had been delegated to collect the contents of mite boxes in certain parts of the country in Ireland. In course of conversation Terna mentioned her late father's cousin who was then working in Africa, a Bishop of South Galway whose missionary priest cousin had been killed by a fall from his motor cycle years before. The subject of ways and means to help the mission cropped up. Out of that the stranger learned of her different features and approved of them ...

At last the husband and wife were able to come and go as they liked, so they began to look up old friends who had not even written for years, only to find an invitation in the letters. Sometimes the couple would accept or explain politely why they could not. Frequent long-distance travel was out for Terna for two reasons. She never slept at all during long absences from home, and not for a week after she returned. From then on, indefinitely, she never had to turn left or right until she fell into a deep sleep. That was always the way.

Though Peter was enjoying every minute of his retirement, he sometimes found that he had too much time on his hands. So he took a piece of ground outside the town to keep him occupied on long days. The spot proved to be productive enough after he cleaned it and brought it to a good tilth. Pests were troublesome during the growing season, but he soon overcame that by applying powder and baits.

As the Cannings had had a long rest from the births, marriages and deaths cycle, a slight sense of self-sufficiency was creeping in. And they tended to shut out anything that caused them pain, forget it in the new tenor of their lives. They had only to wish it and it was gratified. Vane was not growing better and they might as well indulge themselves, they were resigned and sacrificial for far too long on the planet of men. To half conform was to half rebel, anyway. Self meant self with them until one morning Terna faced Peter across the table. 'All those extras that we can do without, Peter!'

'Ah! It is too late in life to talk that way,' he answered. 'There were so many things denied us through life!'

'All the same,' she went on, 'our old natures are going to assert themselves again, I know.' So soon they doubled their donations to charitable purposes and she went without the things that she had taken for granted for so long. And Peter cashed in. Once again they found that the joy of giving was greater than that of receiving. From the heights of satisfaction, one of the two then stood like something that the sea had given up. It was Terna. The one who saw far into the future and who had assessed themselves, had good reason to assess another all over again. Jay's health was plainly failing and it showed in his disposition at every turn. His general behaviour became more puzzling, unpredictable.

The woman of faith hoped against hope that the condition would pass ... youthful changes, she told herself. Yet she dared not close her eyes to the fact that Jay's nerves were troubling him. The truth made an immediate impact. Even the years of their cushy retirement had to be haunted with the same dose like this ... The doctors had to see Jay to put his parents' mind at ease for once and for all. Blind hoping did no good. On that occasion Jay sat down, oblivious of everything and everybody around him, and answered no questions. So Vane would have new company soon, the brother whom he had called 'Brud' out of affection for him, over fifteen years before when he taught him his Catechism, winning the unstinted praise of their mother. This was something, then, that the parents would never grow used to; it was too much to take, faith or no faith. Would they both survive it? And were the weeks to pass into months and the months into years for Jay as they had done with Vane? The latter was just what happened, a double disappointment for the Cannings. Had not an aimless life been better for Jay than the close confinements of a ward with people as unfortunate as himself? Imagine his fine eyes falling on his mother for the first time after that! And see their parents go about their duties, half numb but Peter willing to carry on for his ruined sons' sakes. As for Terna, in the deep core of her being a faint resignation was beginning to settle again. And the empty house! It was like starting all over again in Glenmark.

Gay and Blitz flew to their parents' side as soon as they heard of the new stroke. Blitz was quite heroic about it but poor Gay said: 'It is like as if our brothers are lost forever.' Her mother thought that her daughter's hope was poor, then, and her faith? And with maternal concern for her, Terna forgot herself. 'We are pilgrims in a pilgrim land and pilgrims have to endure,' was all she could say at last. Then Gay cited similar and sadder cases in Glenmark and all over England that she knew of, while Blitz made a gallant effort to amuse them with her own brand of humour, though rather uncalled for, then. But they were together and Terna rose to the occasion, even singing one of her little lyrics: *On the edge of Nowhere*. Gay thought it typical and tried to enjoy it.

Anything like the sympathy and feeling shown by the Cannings circle could not be imagined. Some rang to say that they had been speaking with Jay over the 'phone; others said there was scarcely anything the matter with him. And his mother's heart fluttered a little when letters began to arrive from him where he would state that 'she had many years to laugh yet'. How she loved those letters! 'Motherhood is just another kind of vigil,' she would say, and feel all better for having said it.

Blitz's subjects grew more and more interesting to her and it was understood that she would devote her life to study outside working hours. She mentioned attending the play, *Brand*, in the Oxford Playhouse before she left London, and recalled acting in it in her Galway University days (referred to already) when she had done the part of Brand's mother. She also spoke of a new group associated with the development of concrete poetry. But while she entertained her listeners she knew that her mother's mind was full of the last doctor's words, that 'Vane and Jay suffered from their minds having developed too soon, and further, to quote, 'the boys had over-developed minds and over-refined bodies'. It was a mixed consolation.

# CHAPTER 30

# *Sympathy and Tours*

Weeks after, Terna was buying wool in a store when a woman who had lost all three of her children, and who had become case-hardened as a consequence, touched her shoulder, saying: 'I heard it. I am sorry, Mrs Canning!'

'Thanks,' Terna managed to say before the sympathiser spoke again.

'You'd need another shoulder, but let the ould wurld do its worsht, the besht one is comin' an' ye mighn't be a white martyr much longer.'

An itinerant tourist who happened to be standing near, spoke up: 'If you'll excuse me. Isn't it time you knew it, Ma'am?'

'Knew it? Knew what?' Terna asked, 'What do you wish to say?'

'That when you think it's on your side, it's the other way round. She grinned viciously.

'What — whatever can it be? It?'

'Time, the maker and the breaker.'

'What else? No creature is sure of the next breath. Time is time, and one can't depend on it, with its stings as well as it wings.' Two doubtful types of consolation, the second one a shade vindictive, Terna thought, as she moved away, smiling. She knew the first speaker, a woman of narrow interest, only herself and what the stars foretold. The second was more realist than theorist. On her way back, Terna solemnly decided that whatever was said or done she would not think of, or write, even a couplet, any more. And once home, she hid herself in her nocturnal retreat, not to seek enlightenment, but to consider and reconsider the regrettable turn of events. Again she closed her eyes so as to have the double delight of detachment. Nor did she think of the darkness as being mystically clarifying that night or holding anything exclusively for her, yet she stayed, blank and satisfied, until a few chilly drops fell from a drooping branch when it was stirred by a speeding current of air.

Then someone emerged from the house, mounted the steps and called, in an educated voice, 'M-a-t-e-r M-e-a,' and the voice had concern in it. Blitz had followed her out to suggest something and they walked in together, Terna still holding the parcel of wool.

'What is it, Blitz?'

'Why don't we clear off somewhere to spite our sorrows?' her daughter asked.

'Well said, Blitz! Dad's antidote again, a reliable one,' Gay announced.

And Peter, who was reading a certain item in a paper in a deep chair, smiled at them and said with his eyes still on the paper, 'Well, here you are! Listen,' and he soon packed the three of them off to the Wexford Festival, the Opera *Orfeo and Eurydice*, on the time of strikes in Ireland, on a date in 1977. Surely the journey was something worth while, and when it was followed by a run in Wexford, Terna began to throw off a threatening inertia, and Gay and herself drove around while Blitz spent some time with the poet Michael Hartnett, who had risen from postman, to telephonist, to M.Litt., Trinity College, Dublin, as well as columnist in *Hibernia*. Blitz admired him very much.

On their homeward journey they visited Vane and Jay and found them still unchanged, but looking better. And on the way home Gay surprised her mother by suggesting that it would be better if Blitz returned to Ireland to work and study so she could be near her parents. After another day, Gay and Blitz flew to London, Blitz intending to spend a night in her sister's place. Trouble was telling on Peter from that on, and Terna made it a point to serve most of his favourite dishes. The recipe for a chicken:

Brown a chicken slowly in 1 oz. of butter with 1 oz. of oil. Place it in a warm casserole. Add 1 sliced onion, 1 crushed garlic clove, and a medium sized tomato, 1 seeded, sliced green pepper, ½lb. of small mushrooms. Add a small glass of white wine (or cider) to the casserole. Cover and cook, gas mark 5-4, for 1½ hours to 1¾, depending on size. Allow 20 minutes per lb., with twenty minutes extra.

How Peter relished it when it was served on hot plates in a heated room! There were certainly days of pressures for him from that period on. And the Winter dragged that year. And though the family kept in touch all the time, the parents experienced a terrific feeling of emptiness until the first bulbs of the next year braved the weather and appeared over ground. An optical treat for the woman of sanguine disposition! Following the last blooms of the earlier Christmas roses, in order of flowering came the first sign of snowdrops with their partly pendent green and white heads.

'Aren't they like happy messengers, Peter?'

'Messengers?'

'Yes, mute messengers of the imagination. And maybe not.' She brightened.

'Either way we have often felt worse than we do now.' He nodded as she went on:

'Right. And the rest of our time can be just a quiet venture for us. To remain interested and even curious is the whole thing. A healthy curiosity is an investment in well-being, and we have only one span of life, unlike the perennials, snowdrops that bloom annually.' They were in the garden, then, leaning over the beds that were to gladden them as the weeks went by. Crocuses with different slight touches of colour showing, daffodils, tulips and the slender grape hyacinths. Terna expected a great show because the flowers had naturalized and multiplied over a long term when the soil was suitable for those marvels of Nature. The grey beams of a still wintry sun fell around them but they had no effect on the plants that were not showing. The man and woman walked around in silence. Then Terna said suddenly: 'I am so forgetful, Peter! Gay said on the way home from the Festival that Blitz should come to Ireland, to be nearer.'

'Oh! Gay? And Blitz? What did she say to that?'

'She seemed to be in agreement,' she told him.

'I am surprised. Blitz would never – decide –'

'To leave London? Yes, she would, as it is she strives to see us quite often as well as her sick brothers.'

'Terna, that is too good a thing to happen.'

Then he asked her what she was writing next, in a concentrated tone. She turned away with a short laugh that held something that did not hide her disinclination.

'I – I would not care if I never committed another syllable to paper.'

'Oh! but you would, Terna! Don't tell me that. It's not that you're emotionally drained or that the ideas do not come, but you are disappointed, different to the times when you wrote about happiness and gratitude.' She was not moved. 'You intended to write a short story. You were discussing techniques, you remember. How is it done?' Just to be kind, she grew more mellow.

'A moment of time, perception, a single incident to build on, and anything from 2,500 words to 50,000.' Then she added, as if getting it over and done with, 'It's the Joycean method.' Then more amiably, 'And like a play or poem, the story must be kept moving.'

Peter was very kind as they went into the house to eat something and he was very serious when he said that they both should have a holiday in a warmer climate. Poor Peter! He had a fixed idea as to the value of a change of scene and people as the answer to everything. But Terna was not in the mood. They talked of current features, of the Community efforts and the activities of an amateur Dramatic Society's production in the unpretentious twin parish of Garmount within three miles of them. Peter had not a burning interest in drama, either amateur or professional, at any time. In these days, between decision and indecision and on arriving at a conclusion, the couple would often finish up on the solid comfort of their fireside chairs, even though the fact of their sons' illness was forever before their minds. And when Peter buried himself in a story, she thought of a few lines of a French verse that she had learned in youth, and applied them to their sons in their plight:

> Au banquet de la vie, infortune convive,
> J'apparais un jour et Je meur,
> Je meur, et sur ma tombe
> Où lentement J'arrive
> Nul ne viendra pas verser des pleures ...

Her husband took a furtive look at her and he knew it was the time for perfect quiet for she was in one of those not so rare depths of thought where past, present and future met. Her special experiences, her spiritual privileges, were to be treasured as the sombre tranquillity of the hidden world of the dark, the telling dark, the whispering dark ...

The newspapers were full of the pressing unemployment problems when hundreds of school leavers were forced to apply for dole. The Government of the day put that measure into effect in the hope of an improvement in the situation. What was happening then? Young people rushing into marriage without the necessary wherewithal to live on, and being jolted into reality at the first sting of financial insecurity. And in desperate moments, when the picture was really grim, referring to marriage as a mincing machine. When asked for an opinion on the matter Terna thought that people of sixty-five should hand over their jobs to the impecunious younger groups. Living on unearned income could be more or less demoralizing for the work-willing and the able alike, those with an incentive to work.

CHAPTER 31

# *Terna's Interests*

A long time after, Peter had occasion to visit people in the country with whom he had business contacts, so Terna began to look up the reviews on *Halcyon Days* which she had mislaid, unfortunately. The reviews went like this, writing from memory:

I   A critic in Oxford University, who was competent to judge, said that her work showed a keen feeling for the beauties of Nature, and had a charming directness which would go well if it was set to music.

II   The *Connacht Tribune*: 'She draws up images from the earth like Wordsworth, and that the reader thought of Keats' magic casements, and that the verses wanted no other music than their own. Graphic.'

III   The *Herald* described her publication as a gem of its kind.

IV   The review of the *Irish Catholic* is not available either but the word 'optimism' came into it.

Terna was certainly optimistic when she thought in the cool darkness later:

> *I love the night*
> *Held in its sable bands.*
> *All that I see*
> *Is a daylight land.*

But her intense enjoyment was to be short-lived for the hidden moon raced from its moorings in an inky cloud, casting its accustomed glimmer around; and she stood there for moments, not missing the moon's play on the stained glass windows of the church, an approximate two hundred yards from her across a field. But all was dark again overhead for the amber light disappeared with a flash, leaving her motionless as before and staring into the darkness. Finally, she turned home, and it was then that she had good reason to stare, for Blitz was seated on the sofa, smiling and enjoying a cup of coffee. They greeted each other and then Blitz laughed out. As she stood to prepare coffee for her mother she said:

'You did not expect me yet, but wait!' She was breathlessly happy. 'I've been making applications for a post in Ireland.'

'Yes, Blitz! Tell me! Any results?'

'Plenty. Though not all satisfactory. I know what I want.'

'So do I, Blitz! That will be ideal for all of us.'

'And that is not all, *a mháthairín!*\* You have cause for further rejoicing. After one of my regular check-ups, my doctor tells me that I'm in perfect health, as sound as a bell every way,' she added, happily independent.

'Fine, Blitz, that gives me a lift when I should be down.'

After allowing their coffee to grow cold, they finished it. Then Blitz enquired for her father, about his avid interest in world events and if he still showed his natural abhorrence of war and news of war by switching off the radio. Further, Blitz told her that she had seen the tomb of Oliver Goldsmith in the Inner Temple in London and that his tombstone was the shape of a coffin. And there was also a memorial to him in Westminster Abbey.

'He earned it,' her mother said. 'And by the way, I almost forgot, I am told that Vane actually signed his name on receiving his last parcel of goodies.' She smiled hopefully.

'So he is not without some consecutive thought. We have reasons to be happy.' She rose and drew a chair for Blitz while she did the wash-up, feeling renewed and relaxed, really. Then the name of one of her little lyrics crossed her mind, and she darted like a teenager into the next room where she found it on her desk: 'Keep the bells ringing.' She returned quickly with a dainty Aynsley bell that her son-in-law had given her on a visit and began to shake it merrily as she sang. Blitz loved every word and admired her mother's determination to keep going even in that sense. So after ringing and singing,

---

\*   Irish for mother-een.

they had a discussion on pleasure, places and people whom they met in the South of Ireland previously, until they grew drowsy enough to retire early. Not before Blitz had locked her car.

Peter was delighted to see Blitz next morning and more so when she informed him of her plans, to be back in her own country for good. They both emptied the car that was almost bursting at the seams with her books and some other belongings. The rest of her stuff was on the way by lorry and they would have to collect it later when it suited. Terna persuaded her daughter to rest for the next few days, a way the woman had with all long-distance friends, before they all started on their rounds of visiting relatives, attending concerts, poetry readings by Irish poets and poetesses in Trinity College and elsewhere. Peter accompanied them on those outings some of the time, but other times all his masculinity rebelled against the womanly necessity of window shopping, fitting and buying seasonal clothes, all of which took more than a few hours out of a short day.

'This is more like old times,' Terna remarked once after they finished a tour of the shops in Dublin and drove through Cabra on the North side, on to Killiney Hill where there is a splendid view. From there they drove to Portmarknock with three miles of sand, and finally, to the Hill of Howth. On that occasion they also visited Glendalough with its wealth of woody hills. The bed in which Saint Kevin slept is about fifty feet over the Lough or Lake. The cave containing the bed is eight feet deep and four feet wide. After a night in a City, time allowed them only flying visits to Arklow, Wicklow and Greystones – and Bray close to the Dublin mountains and nearer the Wicklow mountains.

When passing through beautiful countryside, Blitz slowed down to call their attention to low bushes clipped to the shape of animals in a garden. 'Awful,' cried Terna, 'it is topiary, and Nature never intend that.' Then they sped on past a shaky structure bridging a dull, muddy steam in boggy land to their right, and it was here that they increased speed so as to see Vane and Jay on the way home to Glenmark. On that late evening, Blitz suddenly asked her mother how she remained so vital, and how she never let her life become complicated. She believed that even if her mother were to become a hopeless invalid that she simply would not let herself slacken.

Blitz paused.

'Have you ever been lonely, Mammy? Here?'

'Oh, yes, yes. But on account of the harmony that we have enjoyed at all times, that other feelings never caught on ... Though a little of it is no harm, not being solitary and without some loneliness I should feel rather impoverished.'

'Oh! there it is. I've heard that before in my travels from people who have lived out most of their lives, and I can't understand how the elderly ones sound so grateful for it.' That was that.

For some reason known to herself, Blitz Canning made a complete clearance of most of the contents of her wardrobe and posted the lot to one of the Gay Byrne charities. The lot included some of her recently acquired garments that had cost so much, even real suede articles as well as Jaeger dresses that she had not yet outgrown. While Terna was wondering about it all, her daughter had started on still another sweep, a dramatic one, of long, medium boots and several pairs of shoes for a local need. The little donor managed to keep a few fairly worn pairs for herself. And being more than a trifle concerned, Terna demanded an explanation. 'Blitz! Whatever are you doing?'

'It is all right, Mammy!' Blitz, the Good, answered with a serious fervour. 'I am only giving what I have received.' She smiled hopefully.

'I'll be togging myself in the latest, shortly. Besides you're forgetting that I have posted five applications for a *suitable* post since I returned from England.'

Peter overheard the earnest tones and said: 'You should not have any difficulty placing yourself. You are a hundred references rolled into one.' Blitz was visibly moved at the words.

'Thanks, Dad! Thanks, Pater Meus!'

'And reliability is your second name, dear!' Terna added, encouraging her.

'That's another reference, Mammie! And now I have to tell you that I have priced a private residence in County Meath and looked at a smaller one. The first place is up at £16,000 and it is sited at the end of a drive with a private entrance. It is eighteen miles from Dublin City. You will love it. It has all the usual amenities. The lawns are beautifully laid out with the monkey-puzzle trees, prickly ones, and other colourful shrubs.' Of course, the description of the scenery enchanted Terna and she could not wait to comment: 'Beautiful! It must be more than beautiful.'

The sale was in progress on the buyer's behalf, with others bidding against her, the solicitor acting for her demanding that she would have early possession. Blitz lived in high hopes and her parents had already chosen their presents for the house-warming, even while she spoke, when her solicitor rang to advise her not to proceed with the purchase of the house and that there was a certain flaw. Blitz was truly disappointed. The dream house was not to be hers, after all, but Peter looked on it as just another deal falling through, and Terna asked herself what her eldest son would have said in the circumstances. 'There is always another house,' he would have told them in the even, good-tempered way of his earlier days.

Before she looked about her again, the young house-hunter went to the Kerry Gaeltacht for a week-end, where she had been received so kindly before by new friends including a lady of ninety years who had just appeared on Irish Television and who attributed her longevity to plain living and hard work.

While her second daughter was absent Terna collected all the replies to her applications. She also travelled to the famous Shrine of the Apparitions once again, with Peter and all the family intentions and Blitz's aspirations at the feet of the heavenly citizen there. Terna knew then that Peter was right, that she *would* write, and the name of the work would be *Candles in the Night*.

'We have boundless faith, Peter, ever and always. Haven't we?' Terna asked.

'*You* have,' he answered quietly.

'And Blitz has great potential, and promises are supposed to be sacred to our spiritual Friends above,' she added. Then she whispered in the shrine-light to the Lady: 'Make Blitz like yourself, so she can talk with your Son.'

The two of them arranged the run so that they could be back and have Blitz's room heated on her return. She had sent a card from the Blasket Islands already. The card arrived the same day as herself for she returned that evening, full of praise for another house that she intended to make her own. She was not to rush things at first or set her heart on owning it yet, as there were so many bidders. The house had all the features of the first one but lacked a drive. That could be managed ...

When Blitz read her replies, she travelled to a Dublin convent to be interviewed as a start. The interview was successful, as were others. But Blitz craved to work and live in the country as a change. For some time she picked up the *Irish Independent* every day with the same idea in mind – a post near her parents. On a certain day as she scanned the teaching posts her eyes fell on her ideal one, a teacher of German and Irish in the Benedictine Monastery of Glenstal Abbey in Murroe, County Limerick. She contacted the headmaster of that place and procured the post immediately though there were over thirty applicants for it. Though it must be repeated that her mind was definitely fixed on drawing nearer home, ultimately.

Nevertheless, Blitz loved the place and described it to a few in detail, as a spot to dream in, a pax-milieu which she loved; and that her very soul responded to its ineffable luxuriance in solitude as it did when she was in Kylemore. She hoped to serve. She also mentioned that her time-table was liberally construed, especially with the un-expected additions of English, Civics and Geography at times. Her lesson preparation could best be termed scanty, her corrections rushed, though she had phenomenal energy of mind. Blitz stated that the school was easily run and that academic standards were neither understressed or overstressed. She thought that the school was sadly understaffed ... and that she looked forward to seeing the Clausaura ... Then she added that she fully counted on writing her life in her spare time the year after with a detailed version of her travels all over the world. Poor Blitz was a revivalist all through.

On her first visit home she was bubbling with well-being. The change from the London confusion and bustle, and later from the little town of five streets, to the rural calm surrounding Murroe and the turreted Glenstal, must have been totally tranquillising for her. She had postcard views of the Abbey church, the belfry, the entrance court and the towers of the Castle.

Oh! it was so, so impressive to hear speak of it! More than once she expressed her surprise at the Reverend Headmaster's vitality. He was always on foot and ever so vigilant of the boys under his care, all of different dispositions and ages, some few problematic.

The month of February 1978 dawned wet, cold and blustery, but there were times when it was mild enough to carry out early operations in the town gardens. Terna, however, postponed this. Instead, she sat down and wrote to different relatives that Peter, Blitz and herself would have ample opportunities to visit them more often as Blitz had taken up teaching in Ireland. The circle looked forward to her daughter's peculiar banter and recalled the whizz-kid magic of her adolescent days. Terna informed Blitz of this. She learned of her cousin's marriage in Rome then, for Terna had heard of it already.

# CHAPTER 32

# Blitz's Movements

Blitz returned in gay spirits and speaking much of duty. Terna was alone once more and, of course, she began to think of the work that was born after a candlelight procession in Knock – *Candles in the Night*.

Verse:

> Candles in the night
> And crowds of people
> With the pilgrim spirit,
> All the time they're in it
> It's candles in the night
>     at Knock.

Chorus:

> Candles in the night,
> The way they're shining
> With a thousand lights,
> And voices rising,
> In the candlelight
>     at Knock
>
> Candles in the night
> Like living symbols,
> In a procession,
> With a hymn at times
>     at Knock

*Candles in the night,*
*A candle in each hand,*
*A torch of burning faith,*
*A visionary sight*
*Of pilgrims on their way*
*at Knock*

*Candles in the night*
*As pilgrims kneel and rise*
*Around the vision grounds,*
† *Waiting for a sign*
\* *In dying candlelight*
*at Knock.*

† (softly)
\* (slowly)

Terna of Carfort felt better when she had completed the stanzas. Then she opened the front door and stood there. From that point she saw the white and red buses on to the Ballyhaunis road; also an Express on its way to Sligo to join the north-bound traffic there. She saw, too, the bare, hilly heights of Gortnalea and the direction of Cloonkeen where there lived some families whose forebears came from Northern Ireland to settle when their lands were taken from them a few generations before, and given to others.

Though the day was cold, Terna, the Thinker, was seized with a curiosity that amounted to longing to see both places where the winds crossed in hill and hollow. She set out and found that Cloonkeen held her interest longest. The appearance of a close grave off a road that was not used much, made her stay around, and it was in this group that she knew another privacy, strictly, that let her take stock of things in her life and family. For a bright moment, as she stood by the leafless trees, her mind was invaded by everything of a pleasant nature that had ever happened to them. Such moments are given.

The winds grew calmer, letting the low music of slow waters reach her from a short distance. The other crises and currents of her life stood out clearly, then. A change. The raw fact of her sons languishing in such surroundings, not knowing for how long, was what caused her most pain, and, in spite of herself, had threatened her faith, even in the face of upholding it to Peter and her daughters. Then she thought out:

*Hope is resignation's child,*
*Nourished on its veiny breast,*
*Ever constant, ever mild,*
*Believing in the future's best.*

The stretch in the evenings was noticeable in that second week of February when Peter and Terna had another run to Dublin by train. Peter had to see his bank manager about business interests. The journey was enjoyable enough but the train was crowded. They had refreshments on the way, and when the train steamed in at Heuston Station at 11.50 a.m. they mounted a No. 24 bus for O'Connell Street where they spent the time until they left for lunch. The menu was tempting. They attended a play in the Abbey Theatre that night where they were warm, in their best suits, Terna's Persian lamb coat like a long muff around her.

On Blitz's next visit home from the school the weather had all the appearance of being broken, not that it rained continuously, but the atmosphere was icy and the roads were unsafe for travelling. That explained why she travelled with friends in their car. She was only being cautious. Not that her Karman Ghia had been giving any trouble, for she had kept it in perfect condition and had it sprayed a week before she started to teach in Limerick. Even a *spot* of rust on the car would cause concern to her. Her short visit was a lively one, for a friend called. Blitz was pleased at the prospect of returning the way she came. The visit ended on a jubilant note for her at a party that lasted long into the night.

There was little or no fragrance in the garden yet, but the snowdrops were now fully open and the daffodils were making a brave show. The not-so-hardy jonquils' leaves were pinched and discoloured from a touch of frost, and what remained of the helleborus were dashed with clayey spots on the leaves. Over in a corner the forsythia had dropped most of its gold and its skeleton branches needed pruning. Terna noticed that a creeper was getting out of bounds and would have to be tied up. Tulips sown in groups the year before, and evenly spaced, were then showing the result of professional planting. Though tulips are poor wind flowers, that particular early clump proved to be the exception for they withstood the hardest blasts from the different points while they lasted. Feeding is necessary for all growing plants, and how these little friends of the garden reward us, she thought. She laughed at herself then for having tried twice to grow a cedar. Terna came out and on that famishing day, stooped to pluck a different daffodil from each of the many clumps and of equal length, for Blitz's room. Then, as the Angelus rang in the new church, she reminded herself that she was a housewife with a lunch to prepare for her husband and herself. As she came in the back way Peter was reading the leading article in the *Irish Independent* and he lowered it as she entered and fetched a vase from a shelf, putting some water in it and beginning to arrange the flowers in it.

'They're fine, Terna!' he began, 'I know I need not tell you that flowers in a vase should look as if they are growing there.'

'That is it. They are for Blitz's room.'

'Good. If she were here her appreciation would be spilling over. Blitz's gratitude for the merest thing is always so touching!'

'That is true, indeed.' She went quietly up the stairs and he continued reading for a few minutes more, then he rose and placed a kettle of water on the cooker. He was muttering and reckoning as he worked: 'With her temperament, health and outlook, Blitz Canning could live to be a hundred.'

Terna returned shortly after and placed some meat in the roasting tin in the cooker. Then she sat on the sofa with her arms folded. She looked before her for some time as if no longer concerned with cooking. She fidgeted with her rings and her head sank, supported by her thumbs for what seemed an age to her husband. What was she thinking of, he wondered. And as for her, in her own mind she saw him standing there as a man in tune with his environment and taking each day as it came. He was seldom moved by the power and beauty of the acres of heath, by the silent, brown ponds in the Glenmark spaces.

The shapeless February clouds waiting to burst on the already frozen ground of the four Provinces, called forth no comment from him, only:

'The whole country is under ice, seasonable weather.'

'It is well for him,' she thought. Unlike herself, for whether it was from special enlightenment or imagination, she had a constant preoccupation with the possibility that the family would be pruned out that year. She went to the window and looked towards the north of Glenmark where rough pastures shone already like a white sheet bleached whiter under a lightweight of snow ... with the frozen vapour steadily falling in the lifeless gleams of an uncertain sun. The gleams were uncertain, chancy, because of moving, scowling clouds. When she went to the cooker to add the vegetables she remarked that the weather was wicked for motorists.

'Imagine picking one's steps through that freezing region opposite us with the tufts of heath and rushes showing through it, the only guides that one would not fall into the narrow drains around there!' She made dessert and served it piping hot.

After lunch they played records for a while, and, as the outside world was anything but inviting, they had much the same programme for the best part of a week. The colourful houses in the town of five streets stood out more under their slated roofs with a pile of snow. The smaller dwellings appeared larger, and all of them were splashed with slush for a foot high by passers-by.

At the onset of the frightening conditions, the Cannings bought extra rations as a safety measure. Peter spent hours in his room reading or listening to his transistor radio when some tunes would remind him of his late brothers who had been accomplished violinists. Downstairs, Terna was going through intuitive moments as direct as Destiny ... an inescapable cringing, then a sense of expedience ... a spiritual experience without its full impact. She drew off her glasses and held them as she took a few winks. And it was in this attitude that her second daughter found her on her second visit to the happy anchor, the house where she was born in Cane Street, the house that still echoed her childish laughter, songs and music.

The annoying, haunting feelings departed as Terna took her daughter's hands in a warm welcome, though with an instant question on her lips: 'How did you face out on such a day with the treacherous conditions of the roads?'

'Oh! not so treacherous, Mammie! You need never worry about me for I have toured a big part of the world in the same car, without a scratch. Besides, the ice is worse here.' She grew thoughtful. 'It is true that others advised me not to come.' She shrugged happily. 'But so far, so good.' She laughed loudly from the sheer joy of being home again.

Peter hurried downstairs when he heard her laugh and soon three heads were together planning a programme for the weekend once more while Blitz helped herself to juicy bits of beef, mixed vegetables, apple tart and coffee. The date was February 18th, on the gloomiest Saturday of the year.

For some untold reason, Blitz Canning brought home some of the many books which she had purchased previously in Dublin when choosing other works for young classes at The Abbey. By next morning the conditions of the roads had worsened, and that meant that they had to change their plans agreed on. Despite that, they listened to the weather forecast more hopefully all the time. But, by the next evening they found that they had to abandon even their valued visit to Knock Shrine that they always fitted in with visitors. They did not dally and fret, however, but played the piano, sang (including *Candles in the Night* to an air of Terna's) and listened to records of the Masters which Blitz loved so much. They reached the most harmonious heights possible in every way.

# CHAPTER 33

# *Fatality*

Late that night before Terna prepared for bed, she sat on the silk cushion in her room, strangely moved and wondering why Blitz looked so much like an angel. Peter was on the landing looking down when Blitz addressed them from the living room below in a voice that seemed to come from far off. At that moment she stood compact and pleased, with her blonde hair like a deep golden coronet under the light. 'You – are – two – Saints,' she breathed, and Terna wished to hear that voice again that held some heavenly emotion in it as she descended to the hall and looked in when her daughter fixed her eyes on her. Then Blitz spoke over her shoulder with a certain diffidence that was unusual for her: 'Saints,' she repeated softly before Terna spoke.

'That is you, Blitz, and it must be a very beautiful feeling.' Blitz smiled with disbelief. 'You have all the appearance of that and of a good, good girl,' her mother went on. And Blitz said slowly: 'Thanks. I often wonder how people can persist in doing wrong things all through their lives.'

This was distinct and apart, and her mother was puzzled, so she reminded Blitz that the judgement of human affairs was beyond human understanding. And having said that, she returned to her room with Blitz following and saying sweetly: 'I will go to bed now,' and again some unspeakable aspect about her was nearly enough to drive Terna out of the house.

It was already near dawn on Monday when they slept and Blitz had to rise very early to be at her German class at 9.30 a.m. Imagine her surprise to see that it had thawed a little during the night and that the atmosphere was not quite so cold, though more snow had fallen.

When she had dressed and eaten she ran upstairs with the same moving appearance, as Terna passed to a window and looked through the lace curtains at the small banks of snow on the sides of the street below; the guttery piles of slush in the middle and the tracks of late pedestrians. In the garden, the rhododendrons drooped under their white layer, and Blitz remarked: 'I love snow.'

'Yes, Blitz!' Terna said and warned her almost hotly, 'You must not travel today. We'll-be-collecting-you-on-the-road', she added, strained and urgent.

Blitz smiled quietly at her. 'You can't be serious, Mammie! I've been driving twelve years and never had an accident, not even a skid. Dress up and come with me and you can stay at a hotel in Limerick until I drive down and call for you at the weekend, and come home.' Terna considered the proposal, even opening a wardrobe to take out a coat. 'I'll need a fur coat,' she began, and there and then she pushed the door shut as if some invisible hand slid over hers.

'I – I – shall not go, Blitz,' she cried, 'not until the days are finer.' Then she begged: 'You stay where you are for today!'

'I have radial tyres, you forget,' Blitz put in. 'Do not worry.'

Then Blitz turned slowly and thoughtfully to her father and she said half in English and half in Latin, 'Poor Pater Meus! Goodbye, Pater Meus!'

For an instant she waited near him, then, when he had said the words, 'Goodbye, Blitz!!', Terna added with a maternal solicitude, almost prayerful: 'Mind yourself, mind yourself!' as Blitz went into the car, saying: 'I'll be home on March 14th.' And she waved with a typical turn of mimicry to make her mother laugh before she moved off.

At about 8.30 Peter rose and helped Terna to prepare breakfast, so that they could fast an hour before the 10 o'clock Mass they intended to offer for Blitz's safety on the hundred plus miles journey. 'I believe that all is well with her,' Peter announced as he left to buy a paper in the newsagent's down the street. 'I hope you're right,' Terna said as he went. He appeared later on the doormat looking so leisurely, composed and happy, more so than he had been in years, that Terna knew a grateful quickening of the spirit that she was never to experience again that day or for years of days after.

Peter read the political news for her, then the financial column in detail and other relevant features. He sat looking into space until a firm knock on the hall door recalled him to the present and he answered it, only to greet a Garda messenger who had to prepare himself before he imparted the sad news of Blitz having been involved in a collision within six miles of Limerick City; of her removal to a hospital by ambulance and of having been operated on, and being in an intensive ward there.

The hospital confirmed soon after that Blitz's collar bone was broken and that she had inter-cranial injuries, multiple cuts. The Karman Ghia was a write-off.

The parents grew numb, knowing that her chances of recovery were slight. Another phone call confirmed that the operation was successful but that she was unconscious. Those hours could only be described by the people who endured them. Unfortunately, there was a Post Office strike on and only serious calls were dealt with. Terna dreaded every turn of the wheels on that dangerous route, going and coming. And passing the scene of the accident that had often been described as 'the highway of death,' the mother would say to her husband: 'Weather it, Peter! Faith can work miracles.' Blitz, the Bright and the Good, lingered for some hours with oxygen, then finally fell into a coma and died on Tuesday night at 11.15 p.m. February 21st, 1978. Terna had never thought in the Shrine light ... or had she?

After all the suspense and having been hopeful and hopeless alter-nately, Terna and Peter had to face the reality of her death. 'It would be harder to bear it if we were selfish, Peter!' she said. Two days later, two Benedictine priests celebrated Mass for Blitz in her own parish church and she was interred in a new grave.

In a homily at the Requiem Mass, the words were:

'Rather than speak directly of Blitz who was, I know, ready to meet her Saviour, we shall focus our attention on that mystery of life and death which no longer holds its secrets for her, and reflect (as she might have done herself) on where she is now in the light of an Irish saying about the dead that would have appealed to one who loved Irish and the wisdom of its traditional sayings, *Tá sí ar shligh na fírinne* – she is on the way of truth. She is now walking the road of truth. What does this mean? It means that the fever of life is over, all life's puzzles have been resolved, the riddle of her own sudden death is no longer a riddle, bewilderment is no more. Blitz has come to a sort of clearing in the woods, in the maze of existence, where suddenly all is light, where her own role in time, in life's intricate web, as daughter and teacher, is clear to her: she now sees why she has been snatched from among us, why her work in life was of such relatively brief duration. What seems to us unqualified tragedy, is for her an open book in which her purpose in life and death is marvellously clear, her new relationship with her parents and family revealed, her enquiring mind and abiding sense of wonder now amply and finally satisfied. All this is what it means to have found the truth, to see things as they really are.

'It is as if the obscure corners of the pictures of life, like any restored painting, are suddenly bright, the true face of the portrait is revealed, the shadows and the shades rise like a wintry mist from the plain and the perfect landscape is revealed in all its beauty and harmony. And from this vantage point of clear and perfect sight, I'm sure that Blitz wishes and prays that understanding may be given to her family and friends, too, to us who miss and mourn her. We cannot hope to see clearly how God can bring good out of overwhelming sorrow, out of the severing of the bonds of family life, but that His will is certain, and that we have a role to play in the unfolding of that certainty is also certain, by building up a framework of support and helpfulness here that will allow life to continue with as much serenity and normality as possible. And yet remain bewildered ... the full truth eludes us but we know that there will be a day of shared truth for all of us, a day when the elect, those who have tried earnestly, however fitfully and less than successfully at times, to live in the light of Christ's teaching, will be gathered from the ends of the earth to celebrate and share Christ's triumph, His victory over death, His and our Resurrection. This will be the day when families will be remade, children reunited with parents, husbands with wives, the day when we shall see our God as He is and realise the immensity of His love and care for us, despite the many strange signs to the contrary that are strewn on the path of every human through Life. Until that day of truth for all of us, I pray that Blitz's family may find in God what they have for the moment lost, and until that day may she rest in perfect peace and in the contemplation of the truth she loved and sought so constantly and sincerely.'

Relatives of both sides attended the obsequies, and one of her wreaths was from her ailing brothers with the words: 'We shall meet at the Resurrection.' At the end of a few weeks her parents had received around two hundred messages of sympathy. Terna's eldest sister came off and on. Terna observed a period of seven months' mourning until a friend advised her to get out of it as quickly as she could.

Some touching tributes were paid to Blitz both in Ireland and outside by her language teachers, and young men who had become converts to Catholicism in the hope of her marrying them, expressed their feelings of deep loss at her death. So the months passed slowly by, and once again, Terna and Peter strove to pick up the threads of their lives by keeping occupied. Nothing would ever compensate them for the irreparable loss of their daughter, and never would she be forgotten for a moment, their first waking thought to night's repose.

Gay and her husband eased their sorrow by seeing *her* parents more often and inviting them to their home. And Jay was most comforting, too.

'It had to happen,' he said again and again. 'No one can dodge death.' There are things that are beyond human endurance, but Terna's personal courage and attitudes stood to her and helped Peter to come to terms with just another cross and never to grow bitter. She was aware that there was an element of bravery in the most timid souls that eventually leads to a relieving realism ...

And the house in Cane Street was just a place to live, sleep and eat. There was only instrumental music that grated, somewhat. Darkness and daylight were just periods of time, and the little pink room of old a faint memory like a disused alley ...

Terna's natural interests in literary pursuits never really flagged though she thought less and wrote stinted phrases, such as the lines on: *Death*.

> *Death, the throttler touches glazy eyes*
> *as a soul passes through its iron door.*

Flowing prose appealed mostly to her then, with interesting variants when she could concentrate. 'Life must go on,' she mused, on a day of cold fog and nippy winds as she crossed over to her shopping reminder and took note of what she required. On her way to the grocer shortly after, she was hailed by a doleful voice and faced a woman of about fifty, galloping more than running, after her. Well bloated, the speaker paused to get her wind, and then went on: 'Well, there y'are! An' aren't ya great to be in it?' She grabbed Terna's hand while her great, compassionate eyes filled with tears. 'I meant to call for months, but women say more when they meet, ya know. They call you a soldier, an' I made your trouble me own, since, Mrs! Lave it so, now, an' get into takin' a dhrop like *I* do, 'Twill keep ya goin'.' She was hurt and aggravated.

'Thanks Mrs!' Terna gasped, and the speaker continued, 'No say at all for us: That's the way for ya. Goin' back to what I was sayin', the last bout of it ought to make a right martyr o' ya.' Terna fidgeted and did not remark on anything until the other woman threw an eye on a pub opposite the grocer's and pressed her to have a *dhrink*. Moving off, Terna thanked her again but did not accept ... she was glad to get away from the eternal reminders.

When Terna was defrosting the fridge in the afternoon days later the thought that had been so much on her mind of late, occurred again; Blitz's First Anniversary was only six weeks away. So, when all was in readiness below stairs and Peter had left for some messages, she hid herself in her cosy room and waited for her mental processes to get into gear, and then:

*February Snowdrops*

*February Snowdrops*
*In crystal beauty shine*
*On a sad and sacred spot*
*Where dearest Blitzie lies.*
*White as Snowdrop petals*
*On February snow,*
*Wrapped in the white of angels*
*She left us here below.*
*She used to say when night was run:*
*'Morning, God! I thank you*
*For the glory of the sun,*
*And for the health I have*
*To get my duty done!'*
*The morning smiles as ever,*
*The sun is dipped in gold,*
*And she herself is happier*
*Within the angel fold.*
*Now all her thoughts are prayers,*

*No stress disturbs her soul;*
*The Joy of God she shares*
*And needs no other goal.*

The past links up with the present now. The book-lined walls of their late daughter's room, of Terna's room and every other available space, bulge with photographs of favourite geniuses and those of other countries, including their own.

Gay and George are home and the place rings with his rich singing of every type of song, even *Abide with Me*, by Reverend Francis Lyte, his gifted ancestor. Terna is seeing the amusing side, too, for George is also engaged regulating the chimney clock which she has neglected to wind for months; and he also adjusts four tiny music boxes, so that the room is full of different tinklings of *The Blue Danube, Return to Sorrento*, and a waltz tune. And, to complete it, Gay's new gift of a windmill-type of music box is being set in motion to drown the others on the top of the piano.

Despite the melody and the gaiety, Terna misses the happiest links, her other children; and her pets, Luxo and her last cat, Peppy, buried under the spreading branches of the old, ash tree.

The same applies to Peter, and they are determined never to keep another pet.

Their English son-in-law understands their mood, so he fixes their corgi in Sylvag Ware near the mirror on the sideboard and opposite a framed picture of Luxo. From the way he arranges them there appear to be three Corgis staring at each other and all ready to tear each other's eyes out.

After that Terna goes to Blitz's room. She stands by the door and looks out at the night. The serene lights of Cane Street shine on the furniture, on the long list of titles of Terna's work, in red and green, covered with cellophane, and the volumes on the orderly shelves; and the frosty stars stare in their settings. Terna sits, loving the stillness and the warmth of kinship at once, and she asks herself if they shall ever have the pleasure of conveying the whole contents of their house to the place that they hope for and count on, and whether their sons who had been blighted before they bloomed may be permitted to return and take up where they left off. All the answers are in the future for the Cannings. All the petty tyrannies, the complexes and jolts of commonplace living must be, and, in the meantime, Terna of Carfort does not indulge in self-pity, but is, simply *a woman of faith*.

# The End

LILY O'REILLY
1978